The hero of the year is *Dr. Richard H. Thorndyke*, the new director of California's world-famous Psycho-Neurotic Institute for the Very, *Very* Nervous—an institute that boasts a highly sinister staff and some very mysterious patients.

Who but the acclaimed, Nobel prize-winning Dr. Richard H. Thorndyke (as played by Mel Brooks) could conduct a psychiatric symposium that falls to pieces when its members are embarrassed by the presence of two little girls?

Who but the noted Dr. Thorndyke could clinically and quietly explain the dynamics of *High Anxiety* (fear of falling) and yet privately suffer from it so badly that he cannot go more than three stories high without having a severe attack.

HIGH ANXIETY—THE MAJOR COMIC NOVEL SOON TO BE ANOTHER MEL BROOKS FILM CLASSIC

Plus a preview of 25 photographs!

HIGH ANXIETY

by

Mel Brooks
Ron Clark
Rudy DeLuca
Barry Levinson

Novelization by

Robert H. Pilpel

ace books

A Division of Charter Communications Inc.
A GROSSET & DUNLAP COMPANY
1120 Avenue of the Americas
New York, New York 10036

HIGH ANXIETY

An ACE Book

First Ace Printing: October 1977

Published simultaneously in Canada

Printed in U.S.A.

HIGH ANXIETY

CHAPTER I

My name is Richard H. Thorndyke and I am a psychiatrist. It makes me proud and happy to be able to say that because, even as a young boy, I always cherished the dream of becoming a doctor. Long before I took my first biology course in high school, in fact, my commitment to a life in the medical profession was firm and unalterable. I never minded studying harder than the rest of my classmates. I never shied away from the more difficult courses. Anything that had to be done to prepare me for the work I had chosen in life I did cheerfully, happy in the knowledge that I was taking another step toward the goal that I valued so much.

In the autumn of 1948 I entered Johns Hopkins University in Baltimore, and there I spent eight strenuous but fulfilling years getting my degrees in science and medicine. Then it was off to Bellevue in New York

City for my psychiatric internship and to Massachusetts General Hospital in Boston for my residency. During these years of preparation I began to do research on the use of drugs in the treatment of psychosis, and after completing my residency I accepted an associate professorship at Dartmouth in order to continue my work in this area. On the strength of the numerous articles that soon began appearing under my name in the professional journals I was offered—and I accepted—a full professorship at Harvard. There I had the great satisfaction of seeing my research and that of several other doctors clear the way for a number of significant breakthroughs in the treatment of mental illness. To my surprise and delight these breakthroughs proved important enough to bring me a Nobel Prize at the relatively young age of forty-two.

Alas, over all these years of achievement and recognition lay a dark and threatening cloud. For, ironically enough, I myself during all this time was suffering from a psychological malady that defied the healing efforts of even the most distinguished psychiatric practitioners. The neurosis is referred to, in medical terms, as High Anxiety, and this is the story of how, under the strangest and most sinister circumstances, I finally licked it.

Despite my condition, I was obliged several months ago to fly to Los Angeles, California. I had just resigned my post as a full professor at the Harvard Medical School in order to become the Director of the world-famous Psycho-Neurotic Institute for the Very, *Very* Nervous. The former Director had died rather suddenly, and the Institute's trustees said my presence there was required as soon as possible.

I will try to describe the emotional agony I went through as my DC-10 made its descent into Los Angeles International Airport. This description may give you some idea of how High Anxiety actually *feels*.

Omigod we're losing altitude! No, the ground is gaining altitude! "Ladies and gentlemen the Captain has turned on the No Smoking sign. Please extinguish all smoking materials. Make sure your seatbelts are fastened and your seats in the full upright position in preparation for our arrival in Los Angeles." Omigod! Too fast, too fast! We're dropping like a stone! Vision blurring. Dizzy. Nauseated. Ka-*chock*-ka-*chock*! Oh Lord, why does the landing gear coming *down* always sound like the landing gear breaking *off*? Where's the runway? *Where's the runway*?! We're going to cra——ahhh, there it is. But we're too high! Ka-*thump!* Oh dear God, we bounced! Ka-*thump!* Not enough runway! *Not enough runway!* Reverse thrust! *REVERSE THRUST!!!* We're slowing down. O thank God we're slowing down. I survived. I survived. Oh dear Lord I'm still alive. Thank you. Thank you. Never again.

As you can see, the syndrome is anything but pleasant, and with the passing years it had only gotten worse.

I made my way down the ramp and gratefully noted the feel of solid ground beneath my feet. It was as I was walking towards the arrival gate that I saw the woman. She looked in my direction; her eyes widened wildly, and she began to charge. I stopped in terror as she bore down on me. There was something frenzied about her, something utterly insane. In another second she would be upon me, and I didn't know what to think or do. At the last instant I threw up my arms to protect my face, and she swooped past me and pounced on the little fellow just behind. "Harry! Harry!" she screamed. "I can't believe it's you."

"Raylene, baby!" the little man screamed back, as they embraced and jumped up and down, leaving me with my heart pumping like a pneumatic drill.

After the flight I was nervous enough as it was. I hadn't needed Raylene and Harry to make things worse.

But things would have gotten worse anyway. The airport was vibrating with tension: everyone hurrying, loudspeakers calling, bongs sounding, baggage carts whizzing by. The whole atmosphere intimidated me.

Suddenly a man in a raincoat and a fedora hat was in front of me. "Please come with me," he said, flashing his wallet open and closed.

Dazed and uncertain, I followed him into the nearest

men's room. As soon as we were inside he whipped around and spread open his raincoat. He was wearing shoes, argyle socks and garters—period! "Do you think I'm attractive?" he asked breathily.

I gulped.

"Do you go both ways?" he inquired. "Are you into that?"

"I thought you were a cop!" I gasped. Then I turned and ran out the door.

"*Wait!*" the man shouted as I sprinted down the corridor. "*Let's talk! Let's try to work it out!*"

This sure was one dramatic airport!

I got my trunk from baggage claim and wheeled it out of the terminal. It was very heavy, so I had screwed on rollers to make carrying it unnecessary.

And they say Nobel Prize winners are chosen for political reasons!

As soon as I got outside an odd-looking individual in a chauffeur's uniform started calling my name and snapping pictures of me. I suppose it's not very nice to say that he was odd-looking. I'll say instead that his face reminded me of the bottom half of a bowling pin: all the features were sort of squeezed together in the middle, as if they were trying to hide from his ears.

"Hey, wait a minute," I said, "Who are you?"

"I'm Brophy," he replied. "I work at the Institute. I came to pick you up. I'm going to be your driver and sidekick."

Dr. Richard H. Thorndyke (Mel Brooks) meets Brophy (Ron Carey), his chauffeur and "sidekick."

That was all I needed—a sidekick. But "Oh, good," I said politely, adding out of curiosity, "Why the pictures?"

"I love to take pictures," was Brophy's answer. "I'm very photogenic. I even develop the pictures myself. Got my own darkroom and everything. Here, let me take that trunk."

Now Brophy was not a large individual. In many ways—physically, for example—he was even a small individual. But he obviously had a big person's heart because he courageously set about trying to lift my large heavy trunk into the baggage compartment of the Institute's car. His exertions produced a spectacle that I shall long remember. He went down on one knee and gave the trunk an almost passionate embrace. Then, veins popping, muscles straining, he lifted it ever so slowly off the curb to a height of five or six inches. Sweat beads appeared on his forehead and his chauffeur's cap drooped over his left ear as he swayed and lurched around in a frantic effort to establish his equilibrium. "I got it! I got it! I got it!" he shouted optimistically, as with one heroic and magnificent heave of his shoulders, he dropped it. "I ain't got it," he said with an apologetic sigh.

Nothing daunted, Brophy attacked the trunk again. Again veins popped and muscles strained. Again the trunk rose reluctantly off the pavement to the accompaniment of victorious howls: "It's coming! It's coming! It's coming!" Again Brophy braced himself for the supreme effort. "It's going! It's going!" he yelled, now at a feverish pitch of excitement, and this time, with one mighty thrust of his biceps, he managed to land both himself and the trunk in a heap on the sidewalk. "It's gone," he said.

Things were not going smoothly for my new sidekick. I had to hand it to him though; he was showing no signs of capitulation. He got up off the ground, spit on the palms of his hands, rubbed them together, and whistled loudly for assistance. A skycap quickly appeared, placed my trunk in the car without noticeable effort, and slammed the car trunk shut. "Don't give him too big a tip," Brophy advised me in a sulky whisper. "It wasn't all that heavy."

Away, at last, we went, first north on the San Diego Freeway and then west on the Santa Monica Freeway until we joined State Highway 1 at the coast. It was an unusually clear day for Los Angeles. I could see Mt. Baldy far away to the right and the tip of Anacapa Island across the water on our left. The Santa Monica Mountains loomed up above us as we rode along the coast. Cars zipped by us as Brophy sailed along comfortably at an energy-conscious 55 miles per hour. I had no desire to have him speed up, however. I was enjoying the ride.

"Gee, Doc," Brophy said after a while, "I sure am glad you're taking over as the new head of the asylum. We haven't had a real chief since Dr. Ashley died."

"I just hope I can do as good a job as Ashley did," I said. "He was a brilliant psychiatric innovator."

"Yeah, innovator," Brophy nodded. Apparently my becoming display of humility had been lost on him. "Boy," he said, "when it was announced that you were going to take over, Dr. Montague blew his top." He shot me a knowing glance. "Between me, you, and the steering wheel, I guess Montague figured he had the job neatly tucked away in his back pocket . . . if you get my drift."

I got it. "Hmmmm," I said. "Is that so?"

Brophy assumed a philosophical tone. "Well, after all, you can't blame him. Dr. Montague's been working under Ashley for the last ten years, and then suddenly—*BANG!*"

I jumped about a foot, my nerves being still a little jangly from the plane ride.

"*BANG!*" Brophy continued, "from out of the blue, they go out and get you, a professor from Harvard University . . . No offense, you understand."

"Not at all," I said. "And I'm sorry if I've tread on Montague's hopes and dreams. But frankly I couldn't resist the opportunity to work with real live patients." And real live resentful colleagues too, as things were shaping up. "Working with patients is much more exciting than lecturing in a sterile academic atmosphere, merely theorizing and postulating over the psychiatric dynamics of mental illness."

Brophy was nodding like he had the ague. "That's

what they say, that's what they say," he murmured blankly. I decided then that there was no real percentage in talking shop with him. "Boy, I tell you," he said, snapping out of his momentary daze, "it was a real shock to everybody when Ashley died. The guy was in tip-top shape."

I shrugged. "Well, you never can predict a heart attack."

Brophy looked at me as if I were a yokel. "Heart attack. Ha! Don't make me laugh."

The conversation had suddenly taken an ugly turn. "Brophy, what are you saying?"

He took a deep breath and skrunched up his eyes. "If you ask me," he said in an ominous tone, "I think Dr. Ashley was a victim of . . . foul play."

Oh, God, I thought. What sort of hokey melodrama is he trying to suck me into. "Foul play?" I repeated. "Heh heh. Brophy, I think your imagination is getting the best of you. Let's not forget that you're working in a psychiatric institution, which is conducive to fantasy."

He gave me a meaningful look that implied, Okay, it's your funeral, buster. Then rather quietly he said, "Well, maybe I'm wrong. Maybe I'm wrong."

But as we turned off the Freeway and headed toward the Pacific I heard him mutter to himself, "But I know I'm right."

Frank Brophy was born in Passaic, New Jersey, in 1940. His father drove a truck for the Goldfarb Dairy

Company, and his mother kept house. When Frank was two his parents moved to Brooklyn so that his father, who was an avid Dodger fan, could be within walking distance of Ebbets Field.

Frank had a happy youth. He was not an overly bright or overly athletic boy, but he was good hearted and full of enthusiasm, and his schoolmates viewed him with affection. Occasionally they played jokes on him, as boys will, but more often they regarded him as a sort of mascot, that is, an inferior being, but one to be cherished and protected.

Frank's main interest was, of course, the Brooklyn Dodgers, and every morning during the warm months he would reach eagerly for the *Daily News* and pore over the box scores, the league standings and, above all, the wonderful photographs taken by Barney Stein. He asked for, and received a small camera one Christmas, and then counted the hours until opening day. During the first series of the season against the Giants he tried his camera out, but as there was only one shutter speed, and that $1/50$th of a second, all he got for his troubles was a role of blurs. These pictures did not resemble Barney Stein's at all.

So Brophy began to study photography. *Study* may be too strong a word, but he did devote a lot of time and energy to his hobby and soon became fairly proficient in it.

When he was 16 the Dodgers moved to Los Angeles, and after cursing Walter O'Malley up and down Flatbush Avenue, Brophy's father admitted defeat and moved to Los Angeles as well. There in 1959, Frank graduated from High School. Next to photography, Frank liked driving cars most of all, and so it was only natural that he decided to obtain his chaufferic license. Having done this he proceeded to examine the want ads, and picked up enough work to keep him in pocket money with enough left over for an occasional bleacher seat at Chavez Ravine. In 1970 he applied for the driver's job at the Psycho-Neurotic Institute For The Very, *Very* Nervous. He was a little anxious about working for a mental institution, but the pay was good and the hours were short, and when he realized that he would not have to deal with the patients, only the staff, his contentment was complete.

He had moments, however, when even the staff people seemed a little strange.

CHAPTER II

Whether Brophy was right or wrong about the possibility of foul play there, the Institute itself was fair to behold. On two dozen acres of beautifully landscaped grounds its tastefully designed Spanish-style buildings of stone and red tile commanded a breathtaking view of the blue Pacific, stretching away to the horizon beneath a spangling sun. The on-shore breezes carried with them the faintly spicy smell of salt spray, and it seemed one could almost scent the jasmine and sandalwood of the exotic Indies far away to the west as the dark surface of the great ocean sparkled and danced in the bracing air. Spotted here and there about the property were stands of pine and eucalyptus linked together by spotless walkways of shiny white gravel which wound gracefully among lawns so green and soft-looking that one ached to lie down on them and sleep for years.

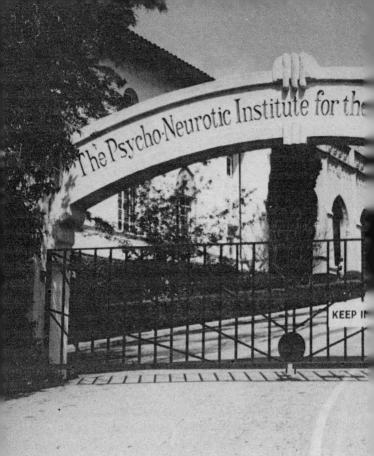

The Institute.

I remember everything about my arrival. Brophy pulled up at the main gate and pressed a button. A soft feminine voice issuing from the metal grating above the button said, "Yes?"

"Brophy here with the new head shrink."

I made a mental note to school my "sidekick" on the finer points of protocol.

The gate opened and we moved up the long circular driveway leading to the Administration Building. With pride and satisfaction I noticed patients strolling easily about the grounds with nurses at their side, only the bathrobes and slippers distinguishing those afflicted from those seeking to ease their pain. My heart felt very full.

We rolled to a stop in front of the main entrance, and Brophy whipped around snappily from the driver's seat to open my door. "Well, Doc, here's your new home." I looked up at the three-story mansion with its gently weathered stone facade and its old watch tower. Above the main entrance a skilled hand had chiselled the words: THE PSYCHO-NEUROTIC INSTITUTE FOR THE VERY, *VERY* NERVOUS. I was impressed by the craftsmanship. It's no easy job to underline something in granite—or to use proper punctuation.

As I was scanning the building's exterior my eye caught a glimpse of two shadowy figures staring down at me from a second-floor window. There were no patients lodged in this area, so the two people had to be staff. I shifted my gaze back to the window to get a better look at them, only now there was nobody there. It gave me a queer feeling, but I shrugged it off. It was only natural, I supposed, for the staff to be curious to see what the new Director looked like.

I walked up the steps and was about to pull open the front door when I was halted by the sound of a familiar cry: "I got it! I got it! I got it!" I stood silently and counted to three. There was a thud, and then the inevitable, "I ain't got it."

Turning again to open the door, I was forestalled by the sudden appearance from inside of one of the staff doctors. He was a few years younger than me and seemed very earnest and cleancut. "Dr. Thorndyke!" he said, "I'm delighted to meet you in person—I've read everything you've ever written on psychiatry: your lectures, your monographs, your books. I'm absolutely thrilled that you're taking over the Institute."

This was an affable fellow.

"Thank you," I said. "Dr. . . . uh . . . uh . . ."

"Wentworth," he replied. "Dr. Philip Wentworth. I've been with the Institute for two years. I just know that things are going to change for the better now that you're here. You see, ever since Dr. Ashley died, there's been sort of a strange. . . ."

He was interrupted by the clank of large keys swinging from a thick iron ring and by the appearance of another doctor, and a nurse to whose waist the key was attached.

Even at that first instant of meeting I sensed some-

Thorndyke meets (left to right) Nurse Diesel (Cloris Leachman), Montague (Harvey Korman) and Wentworth (Dick Van Patten).

thing unnatural and sinister about those two people. The doctor walked with a slight limp, as if he had a sprained ankle, and he was sporting band-aids at rather strange locations on his person: the back of his neck and along the hairline of his right temple. He was well dressed, almost *too* well dressed, and though he looked distinguished there was an air of decadence and perversion about him. He was nearing fifty, had good straight teeth which seemed to be permanently clenched, and rather nasty narrow eyes. "Ah, the eminent Dr. Thorndyke," he said. "It's a great day here at the Institute for the Very, *Very* Nervous." He shot Wentworth a not particularly friendly glance which appeared to make the doctor very very nervous himself. "May I say," he continued, "that we have been looking forward with much anticipation to your arrival. Let me introduce myself—I am Dr. Charles Montague. I was in charge here until *you* showed up."

Montague seemed to experience a moment of gastro-intestinal distress. Then, recovering, he said, "Oh, allow me to introduce Nurse Diesel, my right-hand man. Uh, woman."

Nurse Diesel stepped forward, inducing in me a strong reflex impulse to step back. She was not an easy woman to describe, or to look at. Suffice it to say that if Adolf Eichmann had had a sister, Nurse Diesel is what she would have looked like. Her hair was pulled back so tightly into a bun that I wondered how she could blink her eyes. Her face was all harsh planes and angles, and the rather scrawny build beneath her starched nurse's uniform was topped by strangely large and pointy breasts. They reminded me of rocket nose-cones. "Dr. Thorndyke, how do you do," she said. "I left a complete medical file of everyone in the Institute in your room. I'm sure you'll want to rest a bit and freshen up before you meet the rest of the staff." Her tone seemed to suggest that only a filthy degenerate would not want to. "Dinner is served promptly at eight," she went on, giving a chrome-steel emphasis to the word "promptly." "Those who are late," she announced, "do not get fruit cup."

Coming from her lips it sounded like a sentence of death.

"Excuse me," she said without further ceremony, then turned and walked away.

Rubbing his hands together like the villian in a silent movie, Montague gurgled, "Well, Dr. Thorndyke, may I say. . . ." But he was cut off by a cleaver-toned summons from Nurse Diesel. "Charles!"

"Good-bye," he said abruptly, and hurried away.

Wentworth and I looked at each other. "Do you see what I mean?" he said. "What I'm trying to tell you is . . ." But he too was stopped in mid-sentence by Diesel's arctic hiss. "Wentworth!"

"Good-bye," he said, leaving me standing on my own with only the sound of Brophy's trunk struggles ringing in my ears.

Charlotte Diesel was born in North Platte, Nebraska, the second of three daughters and the fourth of six children, to Marquis Diesel, a brakeman on the Central Pacific Railroad, and Hanna, his wife, on the 16th of October 1939. Her above average intelligence was offset by her slightly below-average physical dexterity, and her reasonably pretty face by her somewhat scrawny figure. In high school she had her share of dateless Saturday nights and adolescent anxieties, but in fair measure, too, she had her taffeta dresses and pink carnations, her gropings and probings and protests and concessions in drive-in movies, her occasional triumphs, and her discouraging failures.

If she had any one especially distinguishing characteristic it was a lack of self-confidence. It was not pathological by any means, but it was more pronounced and protracted than the usual teenage uncertainty. Perhaps it was this limited self-esteem that led Charlotte to choose nursing as her career. As a nurse she could expect to be cast in the role of benefactoress and to be placed among people who were to a certain extent incapacitated and dependent on her for their well-being. Any vague sense of personal deficiency afflicting her would certainly yield to the constant expressions of gratitude and relief that her efforts on behalf of the sick and injured would draw forth. Or so she thought.

As things turned out however, she was one of those unfortunate creatures whose emotionally motivated choice of profession is totally at odds with natural aptitudes and acquired tastes. Charlotte Diesel fainted at the sight of blood, retched at the sight of disease, recoiled from fractures, blanched at burns, fled from injections, and blushed at the sight of certain human organs. Panic-stricken but ashamed to admit failure and mistakes in judgement, Charlotte Diesel cast about frantically for some corner of the nursing profession where one did not have to cope on a daily basis with rampant physical decay and spurting bodily fluids. It was then that she became alive to the possibilities presented by psychiatric nursing: the soft light of the mental wards beckoned to her like beacons in the wilderness.

At first all went well. Charlotte felt that she had been rescued from a fate only slightly less bad than death. The jibberings and hysterics of the mental patients did not bother her one tenth so much as the blood analyses and urinalyses of the sane ones. Some of the patients even managed to display gratitude for a kind word, or affection in return for a sympathetic gesture. Charlotte began to get that warm feeling of benevolence which had lured her to the nursing profession in the first place. Her choice of career seemed to be not such a hideous error after all—until she made the catastrophic mistake of falling in love with one of her patients.

His name was Jeff and he was a paranoid schizophrenic with homicidal tendencies. His problem, broadly speaking, was a mother so possessive and neurotic as to leave him helplessly split between the social demands of adulthood and the emotional re-

quirements that he remain "mamma's darling boy."
Jeff depended on and hated women, and in his saner
moments was so abjectly miserable that Charlotte's
heart went out to him. He brought out all her own
maternal instincts, and her sexual instincts as well, for
Jeff was a very handsome young man. Despite her
training, despite her constant self-reminders to main-
tain her professional attachment, Charlotte found Jeff's
eager and adoring responses to her displays of sym-
pathy irresistible. Soon they were stealing kisses, and
then step by step they perpetrated greater and greater
sexual larcenies.

Charlotte was transported with joy. Through Jeff she
had found someone with whom she could play the
healing angel to the hilt, and have episodes of physical
ecstasy thrown in as a bonus. This was fine as long as
she stuck to the role of healing angel. But, like all
people with sharp limits on their self-esteem, Charlotte
was prone to jealousy. Before long the sight of Jeff
talking to one of the other ward nurses began to gener-
ate acid vapors of suspicion in Charlotte's soul. She
fought them for a time, but eventually succumbed and
began to demand reassurances of her patient's love.
The pressure she put on Jeff called up images of his
dreadful smothering mother, and in not much time at all
he began to identify Charlotte with that hated yet
longed for enemy.

It was only a short step for Jeff from identification to
action. He quickly formed a plan by which he could

have Charlotte's love while humilating and punishing her at the same time. One night when she had the late shift he met her as usual in the privacy of one of the padded cells. It was with indescribable horror as she lay in Jeff's arms that Charlotte saw the dozen leering faces of his wardmates looking in at the door. It was beyond the indescribable what they did to her as Jeff looked on, gurgling and drooling like an ape.

After that night Charlotte Diesel was a different person. Bitter, disillusioned, all her hopes shattered, she swore eternal vengenance. Henceforth she concentrated all her mind and spirit on her profession. She wanted to become the best psychiatric nurse in the nation so that she could get the best jobs with the most power. Once she had that power she would use it, use it to take back from the mentally ill the love and self-respect they had stolen from her. She would show no mercy; she would exploit and humble them; she would destroy. Meanwhile her reputation for diligence, dedication, and efficiency brought her one promotion after another, higher and higher up the ladder, until, from the Psycho-Neurotic Institute For The Very, *Very* Nervous, came the highly coveted offer of the post of Chief Nurse.

Charles Montague was born on Black Tuesday in 1929, the day the Stock Market crashed. It was a bad beginning.

Charles' parents were independently wealthy country squires in Ridgefield, Connecticut, and did not feel the calamity of Depression as most Americans did. In fact, holding most of their capital in the form of agricultural real estate, they benefitted from the crash's effect on the labor market: they had a wider choice of workers whom they could hire at lower wages than they had paid during the Roaring Twenties. Suffering from that peculiar brand of stinginess that afflicts those who have inherited rather than worked for their money, they did not hesitate to pay their hired men as little as possible.

Their only son inherited this singular smallness of spirit in full measure. As an infant and toddler he used to delight in small-scale tortures of animals: pulling cats' tails, dogs' noses, and so on. As he grew older he advanced into more sophisticated pleasures, such as pulling the wings off of flies, or squashing frogs under his heel. As his parents fancied themselves apostles of American egalitarianism, Charles was sent at first to the local Ridgefield public school. There he immediately took on the airs of Lord-of-the-Manor vis-à-vis his classmates, who just as quickly taught him—by overtly physical means—that the economic pecking order of the adult world did not extend to the playground of an elementary school. Charles accordingly returned home one bright autumn afternoon bloody and bruised from head to toe, crying pitifully and eager for revenge. Two of the boys who had pummelled him had fathers who worked for his parents, and

Mr. and Mrs. Montague, greatly outraged at the affront to their son's dignity and to the Montague family's honor, dismissed the boys' fathers that very day. Now the Montagues had been none too popular in Ridgefield to begin with, but this was the last straw, and within a week their house and barn and stables all very mysteriously went up in flames. The local authorities made a show of investigating the causes of the fires, but they had as little love for the Montagues as everyone else in the community, and their inquiries came to nothing.

Still further outraged by this injustice, as they regarded it, the Montagues pocketed their insurance money and moved to New York City where people of their means and outlook could find strength in numbers of Fifth or Park Avenue. Charles was sent to private schools, of course, first in the neighborhood where his parents lived, and then in the prep school belt of central Massachusetts. Charles had learned from his experiences in Ridgefield not to pull rank on his classmates, which was a very good thing, since most of his classmates, financially speaking, now outranked him. He tried his best to achieve some popularity, but his efforts always came across as a form of conniving, and few boys except the social outcasts—the fat, the stupid, the ugly—had any use for him. He was generally considered something of a sissy, having no spirit for the rough and trouble of sports, or for dormitory roughhousing. He was also generally considered rather snide and disagreeable, always ready to make a disparaging comment or a cruel joke at someone else's expense. He got punched in the nose on more than one occasion.

Charles had the customary rich boy's introduction to the female sex, that is, stiffly formal dances with rich girls. However, as he progressed—if progressed is the word—through adolescence, he noticed an odd thing: he was attracted more strongly to girls who were attracted to him least, the fact is, he was never so beguiled by a young lady as when she had contempt for him—and expressed it. For a while this strange inclination of his troubled him, but soon he found it had its advantages. Someone with his personality would never have any trouble finding girls to spit in his face, and someone with his money would never have any trouble finding poorer girls who would be willing to display their contempt for him on a semi-permanent basis, provided he gave them clothes, jewelry, and other gifts in return. He had a happy adolescence.

When it came to a choice of careers, Charles picked the medical profession without hesitation. In what other profession could we have people so completely in one's power, could one inflict pain—"Does this hurt?" or—"Just a series of injections to be on the safe side"—with such perfect freedom and legitimacy. When it came time to choose a speciality, Charles accurately perceived that mental anguish was the most acute of all, and he chose psychiatry so that he could observe mental anguish to the full, and perhaps even contribute to it.

This happy state of affairs was moved by the fact that, after a number of years, no one wanted to give him a hospital position, or act as his patient. He was beginning to feel like an outcast and felt rather desperate for a while. Then, like an angel of mercy, Charlotte Diesel heard of Charles' winning ways. The rest, as they say, is history!

Upstairs in my room I began unpacking. There was something about the atmosphere of the Institute that made me uneasy. I was running the problem over in my head when there came an unexpected knock on the door. "Come in," I said.

The door opened, and there stood my beloved old mentor from medical school. "Thorndyke!" he shouted.

"Professor Little-old-man!" I cried, rushing to him.

"Lillolman," he said, raising his palm to stop me. "It's Lillolman." And I heard him grumble, "Nobody ever gets it right."

"Professor Lillolman!" I cried correctly, and we embraced like father and son.

Dear Professor Lillolman, one of the crucial influences in my life. He was old now, and wizened, and he looked like a dwarf who'd been caught in a juice squeezer.

"Thorndyke! Thorndyke!" he snuffled emotionally. "My best pupil. The best student I ever had." He held me at arms length and gave me that sharp questioning look I remembered so well. "Quickly!" he said. "A patient comes to you. He is suffering from Belldon's Hysteria. He has a seizure in your office. What do you do?"

I had the answer instantly. "Administer two cc's of aqueous thorazene coupled with one cc of somadiozene intra-muscularly."

"And?" Lillolman asked, plainly delighted to be playing our old game again.

"Never take a personal check," I replied like a shot.

Lillolman was jubilant. "That's my pupil. That's my boy. I'm so proud of you. Head of your class at Johns Hopkins. Associate Professor at Dartmouth. Full Professor at Harvard. And now, head of the most prestigious psychiatric institute on the West Coast." He looked at me with great affection, and his kindly old eyes misted over with tears. He turned away. "Excuse me," he said. "When you get old, you get emotional." He sat down and blew his nose loudly into the palms of his hands, an old academic habit of his.

"Can I get you a Kleenex?" I asked.

"Yes, please. I blew too fast."

I gave him a tissue and smiled down at him. He more than anyone else had helped me to become what I am. From the first time I came up to him to ask a question after a lecture in college there was a strong rapport between us, a shared enthusiasm for medicine and psychiatry, an intense drive to push back the frontiers of knowledge. He had seen in me a potential for great things, and had instilled in me a determination to achieve them. And all along the way he had been ready to guide, to advise, to encourage. He was more like my father than my teacher, and it gave me a sharp pang in my heart to see how old and shaky he had become since the last time we'd met. For the first time since I'd known him he seemed frail. "Professor," I said, "It's so good to see you. So good. I had no idea you were working here at the Institute."

He finished wiping his palms and looked up at me with a skeptical expression. "Working is a big word. I'm a consultant. It's a fancy title for a part-time job. I come in two hours a day. I don't bother them. They don't bother me."

He stood up, stretched his cute skinny arms over his head, took a deep breath, and tottered over to the French doors facing the Pacific. "You know, your predecessor, Dr. Ashley, hired me," he said, opening the doors wide and letting in the cool ocean air. He took another deep breath which seemed in some ways a sigh. "It's a shame he died so suddenly. He was going to make some big changes around here." He gazed forlornly out at the panorama of sea and sky. "Look at the view out here, Thorndyke. It's spectacular. Have you seen it?"

I felt my intestines starting to calcify. "No, I've been

unpacking,'' I said, trying to sound casual. "I'll get to it."

"Come look *now*," said Professor Lillolman. "This is the perfect time of day."

I must have sounded too casual. Clenching my teeth and my body, I walked out onto the balcony and looked rigidly up in the sky.

"No, no," said Lillolman. "Look below, down there. Is that a view?"

Slowly, dreading it, I brought my eyes downward—and what they saw was worse than anything I could have possibly imagined. Sweet Yahweh in heaven! There was a sheer one-hundred foot drop between me and the jagged surf-beaten rocks below. *One hundred feet!* Alarm bells went off all over my head. My mouth went dry. My armpits went wet. The all too familiar sensations began flooding through my tortured frame: nausea, dizziness, vision blurring. . . .

Auuuuuuuuuuuggggghhhh! AUUUGGGGGGGGH-HHHHHHH!

"Thorndyke! Thorndyke!" Professor Lillolman was shouting as he tried to pry my fingers off the balcony railing. "Thorndyke! Get hold of yourself!" he yelled again as with one big pull he yanked me loose and sent me reeling back into the room.

For a long moment we stood staring at each other, both of us gasping for air. "Ah, ha," he said at last. "I see that that old High Anxiety still has you in its spell."

It was no good trying to pretend with him; he was one

of the leading authorities on the syndrome. "Yes," I admitted. "It's that old High Anxiety that you know so well."

"Icy fingers up and down your spine?" he asked, starting to check out my symptoms.

"More nausea and blurred vision actually," I replied. "Plus some dizziness and a bit of minor acute terror. But I'm alright now. It's passing. It was just the excitement and tension of taking over this post."

"Bullshit," Lillolman responded avuncularly. "These things don't let go. High Anxiety can be a dangerous enemy. If left unchecked it could cost you your life. I'm going right now to begin a thorough study of your personal file and records. Tomorrow we start our first session of psychoanalysis. Haven't had you on the couch in a long time." He paused to give me an encouraging smile. "Don't worry, dear boy. We'll lick it." He turned and walked toward the door.

Back on the couch, I thought. But I have so much to do, so little time. "Professor Lillolman," I called to him. "Do you really think it's ness—"

"It is ness," he snapped, whipping around and cutting me off. There was that old fire in his eyes, the fire that is ignited in all great healers when they see a fellow creature suffering and in pain. "Don't tell me what's ness," he barked. "I know what's ness. I know my business. These things have a rotten way of lingering and langering." With that he wheeled around, said good-bye over his shoulder, and walked out the door.

I won't deny it; his words disturbed me. One of his words in particular. I turned immediately to the bookshelves to look it up. There we were: lane . . . langley . . . language. There was no langering!

I prayed with all my heart that that didn't mean that dear old Professor Lillolman was beginning to slip.

Fredrich Lillolman was ten years old when the United States declared war on Germany in mid-April, 1917. American patriotism and self-confidence were at their zenith in those years, and Freddy, like all young boys who thought of themselves as "red-blooded," followed the fortunes of the American Expeditionary Force with an all-consuming interest. He was first at the newspaper every morning to read the reports from France and he kept a map with little colored pins on it that showed the positions of the contending armies. So intense was his enthusiasm and his eagerness to partake in the great drama of world war that he often nursed guilty hopes that the fighting would last the eight years he had to get through before reaching military age. Fortunately for mankind these guilty hopes came to nothing, and even Fredrich Lillolman participated in the joyful celebrations which erupted on Armistice Day, 1918.

Lillolman's hometown was Baltimore, Maryland, and among the teachers in the local public schools it soon became general knowledge that the Lillolman boy was marked out for a brilliant academic career. For several years, however, almost until Lillolman's graduation from high school in fact, the direction his brilliant career would take remained unperceived. Then his passion for the Great War still unabated, chanced to read a book by a British doctor who had spent several years of service at the front. The book was called *The Anatomy of Courage* and the doctor was Charles Wilson, who later, as Lord Moran, was to be Winston Churchill's personal physician. *The Anatomy of Courage* was about how man withstood, or failed to withstand the mental strains attendant on trench warfare. It was a highly crucial book in Lillolman's life. He was fascinated beyond measure by the mysterious powers which carried one man through the war shaken but mentally whole and left another to disintegrate under the murderous pressure of constant danger and cold and filth. His young mind resounded with the question, *Why?* What made one man endure while his comrade succumbed? What made one mind strong in the face of stress and another weak? And underneath these questions, Fredrich saw before long, was the more basic question: What made people the way they are? Why is it that one brother becomes a thief while the other becomes a saint? One a leader and another a hanger-on? One a hero and another a coward? Why? Why? Why? Freddy asked. What makes people tick? All he knew about the subject was that he knew nothing, and all that mattered to him was that he should start trying to find something out.

Thorndyke who has just suffered an attack of High Anxiety is aided by his mentor, Prof. Lillolman (Howard Morris).

So when Frederich went to Harvard he studied man. He chose courses in biology, physiology, biochemistry, and psychology—above all psychology. There hardly seemed to be courses enough to provide him with all he wanted to learn. Four years of college were not enough. He went on to medical school, performed his psychiatric internship and residency, underwent analysis, became a teacher and researcher, learned and learned and learned.

By the time he was fifty years old Frederich Lillolman was obliged to admit defeat. The human mind was too vast and complex a mechanism for human beings of Lillolman's generation. Younger men would have to carry on the quest for understanding, and Frederich devoted himself to finding the best of them and guiding them on their way. Among the best of the best was a student whom he "discovered" while teaching at Johns Hopkins. Throughout the rest of his career and on into his years of semi-retirement it was on Richard H. Thorndyke that Lilloman pinned his hopes for the future of the science of the mind.

CHAPTER III

I won't soon forget my first evening at the Institute for the Very, *Very* Nervous. It certainly did nothing to dispell my sense of uneasiness about the place. For one thing, I was finding that it was all just too luxurious. There was gilt and brocade everywhere, the finest hand-made hardwood furniture, Tiffany sterling, Baccarat crystal—everything done in royal style. Quite apart from the fact that so much luxury represented a misuse of the Institute's funds, it was laid on so thick that it smacked very sharply of vulgarity. What was supposed to be a facility for healing the sick looked much more like a turn-of-the-century New Orleans bordello.

I knew it wouldn't be wise to jump right in with criticisms when I'd only just arrived, but I decided it would be a good idea to start asking some gently phrased questions.

At dinner that first evening when we were all having our fruit cup promptly at eight—myself, Nurse Diesel, Wentworth, and three other staff psychiatrists—I decided to delve into the reorganization plans Dr. Ashley had been formulating at the time of his death. "I understand Dr. Ashley was about to make some radical changes here at the Institute. Does anyone have any idea as to what those changes might be?"

Wentworth and the three staff psychiatrists exchanged nervous glances. "Well," Wentworth said finally, "for one thing he wanted to change . . ."

"The drapes," Nurse Diesel interrupted in a tone that reminded me of the chop of a guillotine. She gave Wentworth a blistering look that made him and the other three doctors cringe down in their chairs.

"*What?*" I said, not understanding.

Nurse Diesel regarded me with patient condescension, as though I were cretinous but wealthy. "He wanted to change the drapes," she explained, "the lavender drapes in the psychotic game room."

"Was that the big change he had in mind?" I asked unbelievingly. "The *drapes?*"

Nurse Diesel favored me with an indulgent smile that was roughly as soothing as a fingernail being scraped across the length of a blackboard. "As you know," she said, "Dr. Ashley felt that color has a lot to do with the well-being of emotionally disturbed people."

That seemed plausible enough, almost. "Yes," I said. "I suppose it does . . . to a degree."

At this point Dr. Montague made his appearance. He

was a bit out of breath, having apparently run over from the Schizophrenic Ward in an unsuccessful attempt to be in time for dinner. Without greeting anyone, he hurried to the place set for him just to my left, sat down, picked up his spoon, and prepared to plunge it into the first course. But it was as Nurse Diesel had threatened: his fruit cup had been removed. I've rarely seen such acute disappointment, and there was real bitterness in his voice as he muttered, "Only thirty seconds late." Trying to put a good face on his anguish, he turned casually to Wentworth and asked, "How's the fruit cup tonight?"

"Hmmmm-*hm!*" was the demolishing reply. "Nothing canned. All fresh. Even the pineapple."

"I got a kumquat," one of the other doctors volunteered cheerily.

Out of the corner of my eye I caught sight of Nurse Diesel ostentatiously savoring every morsel of the fruit cup she had left in her bowl, chewing slowly, smacking her lips. It seemed clear that she was deliberately trying to torture poor Montague, but there was something more of arousal than of agony in his tone as he whispered to her, "You're so strict."

I decided then and there that Diesel and Montague would bear watching.

In the midst of this little drama Dr. Wentworth suddenly stood up at his place and raised his glass. "Gentlemen and Nurse Diesel, may I propose a toast to our new leader, Dr. Robert Thorndyke."

They all stood, causing me to blush becomingly.

Diesel and Montague eye Thorndyke suspiciously.

"Long may he reign," said Wentworth, and everybody drank. I should say, rather, everybody raised his glass, because I noticed—though I probably wasn't intended to—that Nurse Diesel did not take so much as a sip.

I thought the general level of tension was lower by the time dinner ended, and with brandy and cigars there was almost a hint of well-being in the air. Even Montague seemed more cheerful. "This is an excellent brandy," he said, bringing his snifter to his nose. "You can tell just by the aroma. It's much better than the brandy we used to have. I have been saying for years it pays to spend more money and get good imported brandy rather than saving a few pennies and buying domestic brandy that simply does not have the body, the fragrance, and the smooth aftertaste of a fine French cognac."

I noticed a few imperfectly stifled yawns around the table.

"I always enjoy brandy that's not too smoky in flavor," Montague went on. "And yet it must manage a retain a character that is bold but never too arrogant or impetuous."

"Who gives a crap?" I heard Nurse Diesel mutter.

Montague's face crumbled like that of a man who has just stepped barefoot on a dog dropping. "Of course, there are some, uh, domestic brands," he stammered on, "that, uh . . . appeal to the, uh . . . whatevers."

I hastened to rescue him from his embarassment. "Tell me, Dr. Montague, I'm curious. What's the rate of patient recovery here at the Institute?"

"Well," he replied, taking on an air of despondency that struck me as rather phony, "we get some remission of symptomology in a fair number of cases, and now and then a severe psychosis will modulate into a less accentuated syndrome, but as far as complete recovery goes, I'd say . . . once in a blue moon."

"Once in a blue moon," I said in genuine amazement.

At this point Nurse Diesel slithered into the conversation. "Unfortunately, Dr. Thorndyke, the recovery rate in a classroom is much higher than it is in real life. We're dealing with sick people here, you understand. *Dangerously sick people!*"

I must say that I didn't like the way she talked down to me. It was disrespectful and unwarranted, and it didn't help matters any that in order to emphasize her point she had jammed her fork into the dining room table, pinning Montague's coat sleeve in the process. In an effort to divert attention from his efforts to free himself, one of the staff psychiatrists turned to me and said, "Oh, Dr. Thorndyke, will you be attending the annual psychiatric convention in San Francisco next week?"

"Yes," I told him. "I think it's important that someone represent our Institute."

Montague, having finally jerked his coat sleeve free,

said rather petulantly, "I was going to go until you showed up. . . ."

But he was interrupted by a sudden *chonk!* which, given the spasm of pain that immediately convulsed his features, could only have come from a Diesel-powered kick in the ankle. "I'm sure you'll have a nice time," he concluded in a choked voice.

"Thank you," I said in some confusion, and as I rose from the table I heard him whisper to Nurse Diesel, "This time I think you broke something."

The disturbing fact was that he was smiling.

Later, upstairs in my bathroom, I tried to calm my sense of uneasiness with a good thorough brushing of my teeth. Ever since I was a child, toothbrushing has been almost a therapy for me, a relaxing happy inter-lude in the day's activities. I stood at the sink and chanted rhythmically in time with the motions of my little toothbrush: "up and down and up and down and side, side, side, side, side. In and out and in and out and side, side, side, side, side."

Suddenly there was an explosion of glass as without any warning at all a really huge rock came crashing through my bathroom window.

I very nearly swallowed my toothbrush, I was so startled, and it took several deep breaths for me to regain my equilibrium. Looking down at the rock, I noticed that there was a sheet of paper tied to it with heavy string. I undid the knot and unfolded the paper.

The note said "WELCOME" in large block letters and was signed in script, "The Violent Ward."

I heard my door open with a bang and Brophy's alarmed voice approaching from the bedroom. "Doc! Doc! Are you all right?" He burst into the bathroom in a state of extreme agitation. "Doc! Doc! Is everything all right? Is everything all right?"

I was touched by his concern, especially since it was clear from the fact that he was barefoot and wore only pants and a T-shirt that he had rushed over from his room in tremendous haste. I pointed at the chunk of stone on the floor. "Someone threw a rock through the window."

Brophy's close-set eyes widened in amazement and indignation. "Geez, look at that," he said. "A guy like that should be put away. Here, let me get rid of this for you."

And before I could stop him he was squatting down with both hands on the rock, muscles straining, veins popping: "I got it! I got it! I got it!"

"Brophy, forget about it," I told him, but the words were no sooner out of my mouth than a blood-curdling scream split the air from close by. Brophy and I stared at each other, momentarily frozen. Then we scrambled madly toward the hallway outside my suite. The scream came again, and Brophy confirmed my own impression, saying, "It's coming from Nurse Diesel's room!"

We raced down the corridor and banged on the door.

Thorndyke is "welcomed" by the violent ward.

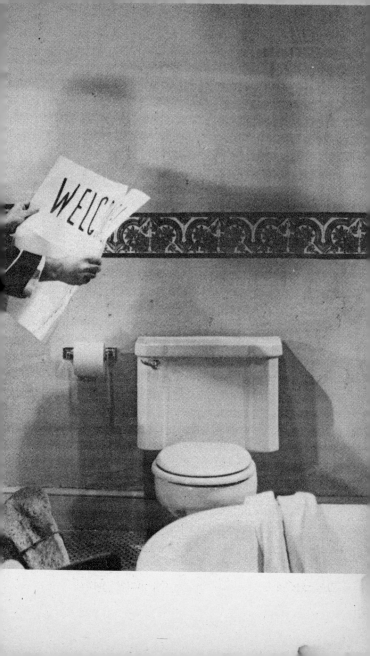

"Is everything all right in there?" I shouted. "Nurse Diesel! Are you all right?"

Suddenly everything was very quiet. After a few seconds Nurse Diesel appeared at the door. "Yes?" she said with a certain haughtiness.

There was something—dare I say it?—mad in her eyes, a sort of trance-like excitement and wildness.

"Forgive us," I panted, "but we heard some weird noises that seemed to enamate from your room."

She looked at us as if we were two half-wits who needed her help to go potty. "Weird noises? Heh heh heh. It was the TV. I'm sorry it disturbed you. I've turned it down."

As she spoke I noticed that Brophy's mouth had dropped open. Following his gaze, my eyes came to rest on Nurse Diesel's legs, which were encased in glossy spike-heeled black patent leather boots that climbed sinuously past her ankles, up her calves, and over her knees before disappearing in the direction of her thighs beneath a loose-fitting bathrobe, which she seemed to have put on rather hastily. As her hands clutched the robe around her I noticed for the first time that her fingernails were unusually long, and I could see that underneath the robe she was wearing an odd-looking purple T-shirt with the words "BORN TO WHIP" stenciled across the top. I guess both Brophy and I must have been staring, for in a tone heavy with contempt, and with her nostrils curling, she said, "Is there anything else, Doctor? It is rather late."

Brophy and I glanced at one another in embarrassment and hastily closed our mouths. "Yeah," said Brophy. "It is late. Good night, Doc."

"Good night, Brophy," I replied, and, turning reluctantly to Nurse Diesel, I said, "I'm so sorry to have disturbed you. Good night."

"Good night," she responded, her door closing as reflections from the ceiling light glinted lewdly off her boots.

Nurse Diesel slides the latch and shoots the bolt on the door, then turns and sensuously wets her lips. Letting her robe fall open, she eagerly crosses her room to the closet and yanks open the door. Inside Dr. Montague is hanging by his wrists from the clothes bar. That is, his wrists are tied to the clothes bar with a thick rope that extends down to a large knot at his ankles, forming a large "V". He is wearing light blue silk pajamas and an expression of impatient anxiety.

"Who was it?" he whispers fiercely.

"It was Thorndyke," Nurse Diesel whispers back. "You're making too much noise!"

Montague attempts to shrug his shoulders, but it is not an easy thing to do in his position. He ends up simply flapping his hands in exasperation. "I can't help it," he says. "You're hurting me. You're going too hard tonight." He looks at her hands with a gaze of mixed fear and delight. "I want you to cut your nails," he says without conviction.

Diesel and Montague practice Bondage and Discipline.

Nurse Diesel smiles a terrible evil smile, half sneer, half snarl. "Come on," *she says,* "I know you better than you know yourself. You live for bondage and discipline."

She reaches out and, savoring each moment, carefully pinches Montague on the neck.

"No!" *he screams.*

She reaches down and pinches him on the chest.

"No!" *he screams again.*

She reaches out yet a third time, takes some skin on his stomach between her fingers, and slowly applies the pressure.

"No," *he screams at the top of his voice.* "Too much bondage. Not enough discipline!"

She lets him go, and her smile grows more terrible than ever as she moves to his side. She lifts her hand up into the air and then brings it down hard on his buttocks, again! and again! and again! faster and harder, until she is spanking him so violently that she is perspiring from the effort.

"Yes! Yes!" *Dr. Montague cries.* "I'm so happy!"

CHAPTER IV

My first full day at the Institute for the Very, *Very* Nervous was very full indeed. I rose at six and was at my desk by seven-thirty. I worked solidly for several hours on the case history files. A number of them made for very disturbing reading, and I asked my secretary, Miss Stein, to inform Dr. Montague that I wanted to see him at eleven o'clock. While I was awaiting his appearance I had a rather odd experience. A small beam of reflected light, as from a hand-held pocket mirror, began to flicker and dance across my face. I moved my head, but it seemed to follow me, almost as if someone were trying to attract my attention. I was just about to go to the window and look for the source of the flickers when Dr. Montague's presence was announced. The moment he entered the room the light flickers ceased, and I, all unsuspecting, ceased to think about them.

57

"I'm so sorry I'm late," Montague said. "It took a little longer than I had anticipated to complete my rounds this morning."

I motioned him to sit down, and he did so, very very gingerly I thought. "Montague," I said, "I'm a little disturbed."

"Yes, Dr. Thorndyke?" he responded brightly, almost as if the fact that I was disturbed had made his day.

"Yes, I've been studying some of these case histories, and every so often I come across a patient who seems to be functioning in a rational and normal manner. Zachary Cartwright the Third, for instance. His family is paying the Institute twelve thousand dollars a month. According to his files, he should have been discharged months ago."

"Oh these case histories are really so sketchy," Montague sniffed. "They hardly draw a true picture of the patient's psychosis. Cartwright is a perfect example. One moment he's perfectly rational and lucid and the next he's a living looney tune."

I decided to overlook the unprofessional turn of phrase. "Cartwright is just outside," I said. "Would you mind if we examined him together?"

"Mind?" Montague sneered, shifting uneasily in his chair. "Why should I mind? After all, you're in charge here. You can examine anyone you want."

I was a bit taken aback by the near-hysterical intensity of this response, but I let it pass and buzzed Miss Stein to send Mr. Cartwright in.

Dressed in pajamas, a robe, and slippers, Zachary Cartwright was a skinny unassuming little fellow of about fifty who looked like he'd just spent several hours locked in an overnight bag. He was apparently rather fearful of Dr. Montague, whose loud and aggressive "Hello, Zack!" caused him to shrink away like a beaten dog. I asked Cartwright to sit down and gave him a few moments to get comfortable. Then I said, "Tell me, Mr. Cartwright, do you know why you're here at the Institute?"

"Yes," he replied. "I was brought in two years ago suffering from nervous exhaustion. I used to get sharp pains in my neck and I dreamt about werewolves."

"And in the two years you've been here, do you feel that you've made any progress?"

"I never get the pains anymore," Cartwright answered. "And it's been six months since I had a dream about a werewolf."

"Do you feel if you were returned to the community you could function in a happy and normal manner?"

"I think so," said Cartwright, casting a nervous glance toward Montague. "I feel pretty good."

Montague, be it noted, had risen from his chair and begun to pace the room. Absorbed as I was in entering my impressions of Cartwright in the case history file, I neglected to give adequate attention to my colleague's movement.

Now a psychiatrist is in many ways like a detective: he should be alert to everything. That's why I find it hard to forgive myself for not recognizing the significance of Montague's actions. In retrospect it all seems horribly clear: the way he began twisting and stretching a rubber band in his fingers, the way he casually removed a few paper clips from my desk tray, the way he strolled around the office until he was out of my line of sight. It all should have put me on my guard, but I was concentrating so intently on the file and on the question of why a fully cured patient like Cartwright was still being treated as sick that everything else was excluded from my mind. My concentration was so intense, in fact, that when Cartwright suddenly screamed and grabbed his neck it scared the bejeezus out of me. "What on earth is the matter?" I gasped.

"I don't know," said Cartwright, obviously puzzled and upset. "The pain just came back."

Montague bent over from behind me. "You see how unpredictable he is?" he hissed in my ear.

"Maybe he's under some tension," I whispered, and turning to the patient I said, "Now I really want you to relax, Mr. Cartwright."

"I'll try. I'll try," he responded, rubbing his neck.

"You mean," I enquired, "you haven't had this pain for a long time and suddenly it's reoccurred for no apparent reason?"

I heard Montague moving around near the window, still out of my line of sight.

"I don't know what it is," said Cartwright, genuinely perplexed.

"That's interesting," I murmured more than half to

myself, and I started to make a note of what had happened in the file.

"The pain's going away now," Cartwright volunteered. "I feel perfectly . . . Aaaaauuuuggggghhhhhh! Aaaaauuuuuggggghhhhhh!"

I shot out of my chair. "Mr. Cartwright, what is it? Is it the same pain?"

"Yes! Yes! Yes!" he cried in great distress.

I decided to have a close look at Cartwright's neck, and as I started around the desk I had a fleeting impression of Montague taking what appeared to be a set of long sharp-fanged werewolf teeth out of his lab coat pocket, the sort of thing kids buy to scare their friends with on Halloween. Now the human sensory apparatus is not geared to accept input which the brain rejects as impossible. Given my great concern for Cartwright and the unthinkable villainy of what I now know Montague was doing, the split second in which the werewolf teeth were visible passed too quickly for me to register what they were. To be sure, they *looked* like werewolf teeth, but since my brain told me they *could not be* werewolf teeth I simply assumed that my eyes were playing tricks on me. Besides, whatever they were was of secondary importance. My primary concern was for Mr. Cartwright.

"Here," I said to him, "let me examine your neck."

But as I approached him his eyes opened wide in horror and he screamed, *"No! No! Go away! Go away!"*

"It's all right, Mr. Cartwright," I said, trying to

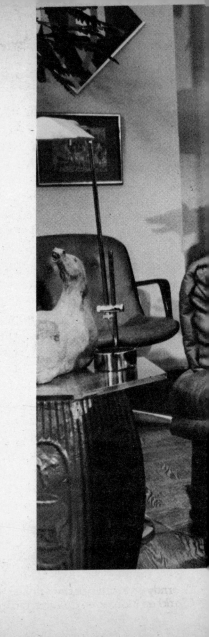

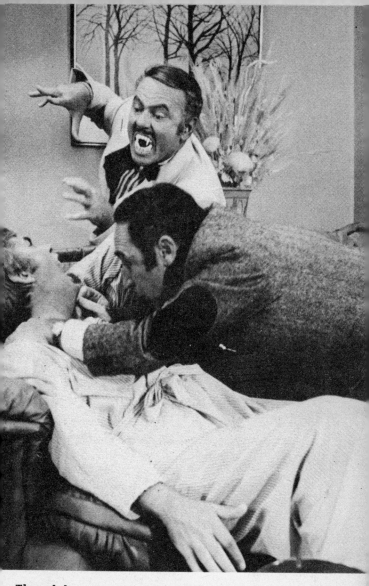

Thorndyke examines patient Zachary Cartwright (Ron Clark) as Montague delivers terrifying coup de grace.

calm him, unaware of Montague's fiendish antics just behind me. "Believe me, I just want to help."

But Cartwright was now beyond help, shrieking and flailing his arms and trying desperately to escape. He made so much noise that two orderlies rushed into the office. "Take him back to his room," I instructed them sadly, watching them wrestle poor Cartwright to the floor. "Give him a sedative and nail some wolfbane over his window."

They carried him out kicking and screaming, and I stood there shaking my head. "I don't understand," I said to Montague, who was standing there shaking *his* head. "It was all so sudden. I've never seen anything like that."

"Sad. Sad," said Montague. "Tears your heart apart."

As he said this, the flickering light I had noticed earlier reappeared and started dancing again around my face. "There's that reflection again," I said. "It seems to be coming from an upper window in one of the wings."

Montague peered outside. "Hmmmm," he said. "I'd say it's coming from the North Wing. Room thirty-five."

"Oh? Who's up there?"

"I think it's a patient named Brisbane."

"Arthur Brisbane? The industrialist? Head of Brisbane Industries?"

Montague seemed suddenly uneasy. "Er . . . yes. I think that's the one."

"How long has he been here?" I asked.

"Oh, about eighteen months."

"I don't remember coming across his name in the files," I said. And in fact I distinctly remembered *not* coming across his name in the files, because the name Arthur Brisbane would have made a strong impression on me if I had. Why, I wondered, had his of all files been the one file missing from the stack Nurse Diesel had left for me—if, indeed, his was the only one missing.

To Montague I said, "I'd like to meet this Brisbane fella this afternoon."

Montague seemed to wince a little. "But he's hopeless. You don't want to meet him."

"I do," I said emphatically.

"Oh very well. As you wish. I'll arrange it for you right away."

He picked up the phone and dialed. "Hello? Nurse Diesel? Dr. Montague here. Dr. Thorndyke would like to visit Arthur Brisbane this afternoon . . . Good . . . Oo-yay oh-knay ut-way oo-tay oo-day. Et it gay?"

He hung up with a little flourish of his wrist, as if Pig Latin were the most natural language for a licensed psychiatrist to use in speaking with a psychiatric nurse. "Everything will be taken care of," he said with a smug smirk, ignoring my astonished gaze. Evidently I was to be left to draw my own conclusions as best I could.

Montague sauntered out of my office while I puzzled over the meaning of: "You know what to do. Gettit?"

What did "gettit" mean? Perhaps I would never know. I certainly couldn't think very well with that flickering little reflection once again jumping and skipping around my face.

CHAPTER V

Right after lunch I had my first session with Dr. Lillolman. Of course, it wasn't really my *first* session. Like all young doctors preparing to be psychiatrists, I had had to go through analysis myself, and dear Dr. Lillolman was the man who had guided me on that voyage of self-discovery. It was hard to believe that twenty years had passed since that momentous first journey into the mind. Back then both Lillolman and I had concluded that my High Anxiety was under control. Now it was clear that we had been guilty of wishful thinking. Even if it had been under control back in those days, it certainly hadn't been cured. We hadn't gotten at the root of it then, but both of us were silently determined to get at the root of it now.

I lay down on the couch in Lillolman's office and let my mind float freely on the gentle billows of his voice as he smoothly and expertly submerged me in a state of hypnosis. Soon, under the influence of hypnotic suggestion, I was re-experiencing all the hideous symptoms of High Anxiety. As wave after wave of panic began to wash over me, I could hear Professor Lillolman's voice coming from what seemed a very long distance away. "Fight it, Thorndyke," he was saying. "Do you hear me? You must fight it. Fight your fear. The only way to overcome High Anxiety is to fight it."

"Humph!" I thought in the middle of my terror. "That's easy for *him* to say." But I was under hypnosis and therefore very suggestible. So as Professor Lillolman kept talking his words began to have an effect. "That's good," he was saying. "Keep it up. Fight it. Fight it. Fight. Fight. Fight."

"Fight. Fight. Fight," I repeated dully, feeling my body begin to move on the couch.

"Good. Good," said Lillolman, his voice rising. "That's it. Fight. Fight."

I felt myself rising to my feet. My hands were turning into battering rams, my arms and legs into pistons. "Good. Good," shouted Lillolman. I could sense him standing near me. "Kill it. Beat it. Fight it. You can win. You can win." He gave me an encouraging slap on the shoulder, and I wheeled around and socked him hard in the bicep. It was strange; in one part of my mind I knew it was Lillolman, but in another part it was a faceless formless monster, a loathsome inchoate creature that was outside me yet somehow part of me, feeding on my heart and spirit, dragging me downward, trying to hurl me into a bottomless black whirlpool of unimaginable fear.

"Good. Good," yelled Lillolman after I hit him. "That's all right. Get all your hostility out."

So I socked him four or five times in the rib cage.

"Good. Good. Go——Hey! Hold it. Hold it. That last one hurt."

"You bet it did," I thought. "But wait till you catch *this* one!" And I belted him right in the gut.

"Okay, that's enough. That's *enough!*" He could dish it out, but he couldn't take it. I tagged him with a left jab and a roundhouse right to the jaw.

"I said that's enough!" he screamed, and I gave him a beautiful uppercut to the heart.

That made him mad. "All right," he said, "you want to fight. I'll give you a fight. I'll give you a fight you'll never forget. Come on. Throw your best punches. Give me your best stuff, you bastard."

The professor started feinting and jabbing, and finally he landed a solid punch. "Ha!" he gloated. "Got a good one in there, didn't I. You didn't expect that, did you, you lousy stink——"

POW! I nailed him with a classic right hook to the ear. He rocked back for a second, rubbed the side of his head, and then said, "Okay. Now you're gonna get it."

And we went at it, hammer and tongs, no holds barred. In one part of my consciousness I heard a knock on Lillolman's door, and shortly afterwards I registered the presence of Dr. Montague. He was shouting "Doctors! Doctors! What's going on here? He tried to get between us, to keep us apart. "Doctors, please!" he cried. "Please break it up." But he must have finally realized that this was an officially sanctioned bout, because he soon got down to business. He warned us a couple of times about hitting below the belt, and on one occasion he threatened to penalize me for butting. Whenever we got in a clinch he was in there like a shot, saying, "All right. All right. They came to see a fight. Break it up. Keep it going."

Somewhere around the eighth round Lillolman got lucky and landed a hard right to my breadbasket. Fortunately I was saved by the bell, and I went to the couch in my corner to lie down. As I lay there I heard two familiar voices. "What happened?" one said. "How did this start?"

"I put him under hypnosis," said the other. "He'll be coming out of it soon. We're having some analytic sessions to help overcome a langering illness—High Anxiety."

"High Anxiety?!" said the first voice, a trace of glee in it. "You mean Dr. Thorndyke is suffering from High Anxiety?"

There was a sound like a giggle or a snigger. Then the second voice said, "It's nothing to giggle or snigger about. And please don't say anything about this to anyone."

"Me?" the first voice protested. "Why should I say anything? Don't be silly. Excuse me."

HIGH ANXIETY

The first voice faded away, though I thought I could hear it faintly calling, "Nurse Diesel! Yoo-hoo! Guess what?"

Then Professor Lillolman passed his hand over my forehead and I came out of the trance. "Wow!" I said. "You'll never believe what I just went through."

"I believe it. I believe it," said Lillolman. "You'll be all right. You're strong." For some reason he rubbed his jaw then, as if it hurt him. "However," he went on, "no more sessions for a little while, eh? I want to finish doing my intensive research on your personal records and case history."

"Fine," I said. And we left it at that.

Later that afternoon, feeling a bit bruised, I went up to the North Wing Violent Ward with Dr. Montague. An orderly with half a moustache let us in through the heavy iron door. Montague introduced me to him. "Norton, this is our new chief, Dr. Thorndyke. He would like to see Mr. Brisbane."

"Certainly," said Norton. "It's a pleasure to meet you, Dr. Thorndyke. Please follow me."

My amazement at seeing a man with half a mustache was rapidly displaced by a feeling of shock as I saw what the Violent Ward was like. Here, in an Institution dedicated to helping people get well, was a virtual dungeon, a throwback to the days of the lunatic asylums, when the mentally ill were treated like rabid dogs and mental illness was regarded as incurable. Doors of solid steel lined the corridor on either side, each of them having a narrow slit through which food—and medicine?—could be passed. The ward was dimly lit, smelly and airless. I had the distinct impression that it wasn't kept clean. Surely no one interested in curing people would lock them up in a place like this. I resolved to act quickly to put an end to such disgraceful conditions. Meanwhile, the mystery of Norton's half-mustache became more and more compelling.

As we walked along the corridor I tried to keep my curiosity in check, but after only a few steps I simply had to ask him. "Excuse me, Norton. I don't mean to pry, but could you please tell me what happened to the other half of your mustache."

"Happy to explain," he said. "As you know, we get some very violent patients in this wing. Well, last week I guess I wasn't on my toes for a second there, and one of them reached out and ripped off half my mustache."

"Oh, that must have been awful," I said, thinking to myself that Norton's rapport with our patients might not be all it should be.

"You'll never know the pain," he responded unstoically.

Just as he spoke, a patient's face appeared in the barred slit of one of the steel doors we were passing. "Norton! Hey, Norton!" he cackled. "See anything that's yours?" He was sporting the other half of the orderly's mustache.

Norton lunged for the face with an obvious intent to kill, but the patient slammed the opening shut before he could get at him. Maniacal taunting laughter followed us down the corridor. My diagnosis was: paranoid schizophrenia complicated by half a Charlie Chan complex.

A few more steps brought us to the cell of Arthur Brisbane. As soon as Norton unlocked, unbolted, unlatched, de-electrified, and disinfected the steel door I sensed something very peculiar. The head of Brisbane Industries appeared to suffer from doggy odor.

He growled softly when he first saw us in the doorway, and when I walked in he started barking and leaning his front hands on my chest.

"Brisbane!" shouted Montague sternly. "Down! No! No! Bad Brisbane! Bad Brisbane!"

"This is Arthur Brisbane? The industrialist?" I asked in amazement as the patient climbed down off me and started sniffing my pants leg.

"Don't worry," Montague said. "He won't bite. Let him smell you. He thinks he's a cocker spaniel."

I put my hand out and Mr. Brisbane started to lick it. "Good dog, good dog," I said, patting him gently on the head. "I mean, good Mr. Brisbane."

Apparently the patting excited him, because he started jumping all over me. "Down!" I said loudly, my years of psychiatric training coming to the rescue. "Down! Sit! Stay!"

Brisbane calmed himself. He started nuzzling my ankle. "Good," I said. "Good boy." And turning to Montague, "This is the most complex psychic phenomenon I've ever seen: the transference from human to animal. It's amazing. Didn't Otto Rank, or was it Kraft-Ebbing, write an interesting paper on a similar case?" I ransacked my brain, trying to recall the specific facts, and I was concentrating so hard that at first I didn't notice the pumping motions Mr. Brisbane had begun to make against my leg. "Let's see," I said. "I believe it occurred in Vienna. The patient suffered from delusions of . . . *Holy Moly! Brisbane! No!*"

Montague quickly intervened. "Down Brisbane! No! No! Down! We don't do that with strangers. Norton, get his leash."

I had nothing further to discuss with the patient, however, so I said, "Never mind. I've seen enough."

As we walked back down the corridor I could hardly bring myself to believe the reality of what I had just witnessed. "Extraordinary," I exclaimed to Montague. "Amazing. How could a poor devil like that have had the wherewithal to contact me by flashing a mirror?"

Montague seemed to have been waiting for that question, and his answer came suspiciously fast. "Well," he said, "cockers are known to be very bright."

CHAPTER VI

*The eyes of Nurse Diesel bespeak death and mutila-
tion as she glares from behind her desk at the cowering
figure of Dr. Philip Wentworth. Her severely starched
nurse's uniform and tightly drawn-back hair are reflected in the monastic sterility of her office, which is
furnished with a half dozen items of the most ruthlessly
geometric and expensive modern furniture. There is a
chrome steel desk topped by a thin slab of polished
mahogany. There are four chrome-steel-and-clear-
plastic chairs, on one of which Wentworth is now
quailing. There is a sofa of chrome-steel and black
leather and a coffee table that matches the desk. The
carpeting is pale gold and the walls and ceiling are a
gaping lifeless white.*

*This office could only belong to a person with one
all-consuming obsession–power! Not a trace of mercy,
morality or human feeling can be found in this decor,*

and Nurse Diesel fits in with it as if she'd been part of
the original design. Sitting implacably in her chair, she
is a specter to freeze the soul, and it is clear that
Wentworth is feeling the chill.

"I swear to God," he rasps, "I won't say a word.
But I can't take it any longer. Just let me leave. Please.
Let me leave!"

Nurse Diesel's nitric-acid eyeballs bore into
Wentworth's anguished skull. "You're just as much a
part of this as the rest of us," she hisses. "No one's
quitting. Do you hear me? No one!"

Wentworth leaps out of his chair in panic, his eyes
wild, his features contorted. "But I can't sleep at
night. What we're doing is wrong! Don't you understand? Wrong!"

Diesel snaps out of her chair and crosses hurriedly
to the window. "Not so loud, you fool," she says in a
fierce whisper. "The window's open."

She pushes it closed, then turns and faces Wentworth, speaking in the tone of a strict schoolteacher
whose patience is now nearly gone. "We have something going here at the Institute for the Very, Very
Nervous that's going to make us all very very rich. And
you're not going to screw things up."

Wentworth is at his wit's end, beside himself with
fear. "But it's against everything I believe in. Everything that's honest and ethical."

Nurse Diesel's lips curl with contempt. "Oh, blow it
out your ass."

"What?" *says Wentworth unbelievingly.*

A sinister change comes over Nurse Diesel's eyes. Her features soften into an attitude of reasonableness and understanding that is as out of place on her face as would be a pair of wings on a snake. "All right. All right," *she says.* "Maybe I've been too harsh. You can leave the Institute this evening."

Wentworth nearly falls to his knees in gratitude. "Oh thank you. Thank you, Nurse Diesel," *he sighs devoutly.* "I'll never say a word to anyone."

"I know you won't," *says Nurse Diesel, running her tongue lasciviously across her sharp white teeth.*

It is evening now as Wentworth drives out the Institute gate. On his face is an expression of joyful release, as if he is beginning at last to awake from a nightmare that has gone on far too long.

The night is black and rain falls in heavy spasms of wind.

Wentworth stops at a traffic signal, his face still radiating relief. In front of his car a man with a black umbrella is crossing the intersection. Without any warning the man suddenly turns and looks directly into Wentworth's eyes. His smile freezes the doctor's heart. It is a smile of doom—horrible inescapable doom.

Then the man is gone, and the light is green.

Wentworth accelerates rapidly. On the steering wheel he can feel that his hands have begun to perspire. "Far away," *he whispers to himself.* "I must get far *away, fast." His foot presses down on the accelerator. The car plunges ahead through the rain and darkness.*

"Gotta stop being so tense," he says as he peers out into the night, and casually, negligently, his right hand strays to the "on" switch of the automobile's radio.

The sound of rock music fills the car's interior, gentle at first, but then noisier and more insistent with each heavy beat.

A flicker of irritation passes over Wentworth's face as he reaches down and presses the button for another station.

Nothing happens.

The music grows louder. The sound of electrically amplified guitars begins to tear at his ears.

Wentworth's hands have begun to sweat again. He pushes another button, then another, but with no result.

A synthesizer joins the cacophony of the guitars. Raucous male voices start shouting out, "Love me, baby! Make me scream!"

Wentworth claws at the tuner, but it will not move. He reaches for the volume control, but it comes off in his hand.

The music is digging into his skull like the fangs of a black widow spider. He swerves off the road and yanks the key out of the ignition.

The music intensifies still more.

"Love me, baby! Make me wail!"

Wentworth stares at the radio in horror, then

reaches frantically for the door handle. He jerks it up and down, but the door does not open. He reaches back to lift the lock button. He cannot move it. He seizes the window handle. It snaps off the door frame like a rotten twig.

"Love me, baby! Make me bleed!" *sings the rock band, its blast of decibels causing the whole car to vibrate.*

Wentworth lurches across to the passenger side, claws at the door and window without success. Panic-stricken he begins pounding on the windows and windshield with his hands, kicking at them with his feet. And the music becomes a searing torture, like molten lead being poured in his earholes.

"Love me, baby! Make me die!" *scream the singers as Wentworth's body suddenly goes into shock and stiffens. His eyes glaze over, and he falls stone-like onto the floor of the car. Small rivulets of blood trickling from his ears gather in little red pools on either side of his lifeless skull.*

The next morning as I was about to depart for San Francisco, Montague broke the news. I'll never forget the shock I felt as we stood in front of the Administration Building and he told me that Wentworth had been found lifeless by the police, having apparently suffered a cerebral hemorrhage and busted eardrums.

"Busted eardrums," I said. "That's a very strange symptom for a cerebral hemorrhage."

Montague shrugged as if to say, so go figure nature. "According to the police surgeon's report, Wentworth suffered a cerebral hemorrhage," he repeated matter-of-factly.

I felt like I had received a physical blow. I couldn't believe it had happened. Why, only the night before I had sat at the same table with Wentworth and eaten dinner.

"I'm not going to San Francisco," I said. "I can't leave the Institute at a time like this."

Diesel and Montague exchanged a flickering glance of uneasiness. "Dr. Thorndyke, there's nothing you can do," Nurse Diesel said, her voice so warm it left me frostbitten. "If we receive any additional information about Wentworth, we'll call you. It's important that you attend the Psychiatric Convention. Remember, you are representing the Institute."

"Enjoy yourself, for God's sake," Montague chimed in with his usual forced good humor. "Get your mind off the Wentworth murder . . . uh, accident, and have a good time."

There had been that familiar *chonk!* sound just after he said "murder." If I'd been watching closely the way I should have been I might have seen the kick. As it was, I could only speculate as to why Montague was holding his left ankle in his hands. "Perhaps you're right," I said to him. "I did spend a great deal of time preparing my speech. Yes, yes, I'd better go. Where's Brophy?"

"Here I am, Doc," he shouted from the top of the steps. "I forgot my camera. Now hold it! Let me get a picture of the three of you."

"Very well, Brophy," I said. "But hurry it up. We have to get a move on."

Brophy got his picture, I got in the car, and after an exchange of good-byes all around we got underway, leaving my two distinguished colleagues to carry on the work of the Institute.

That night, by way of celebration, Nurse Diesel allowed Dr. Montague to try on her new panty hose.

CHAPTER VII

Brophy and I arrived in San Francisco after an uneventful eight-hour drive up the coast. I spent most of the trip polishing my speech for the convention, but often I would find myself gazing out the window, my thoughts on poor Wentworth and the strange goings-on at the Institute. Very little about the place made sense to me. Why, for instance, was Diesel constantly kicking Montague in the ankle, and why wasn't Montague kicking her back? Why had Ashley made such a big fuss about something as minor as his plans to change some drapes? Why had Montague said Wentworth's *murder* when he must have meant his death? Why did Diesel wear black spike-heeled boots to watch television? How had the spaniel-brained Brisbane known about using mirrors to send signals? And what did his signals mean when taken in conjunction with his subsequent behavior?

Thorndyke experiences his first sensation of High Anxiety as the fishbowl elevator above the open lobby begins its swift ascent.

Was Brisbane simply in heat, or was there a less filthy explanation?

So many questions and so few answers! Little did I realize that I was soon going to have more answers than I could begin to cope with.

Convention headquarters in San Francisco was a large modernistic hotel almost twenty stories high built around a central glass-roofed courtyard. By some fiendish miracle of advanced architecture, the hotel was constructed so that each floor facing the courtyard juts *out* into thin air a little farther than the floor just below it. As you stand in the lobby, therefore, you are treated to the impression that the whole building is about to cave in on you. If you leave the lobby and venture upward, on the other hand, you are treated to the impression that gravity will soon bring you and the whole impudent pile of overhangs crashing ignominiously to the ground. The net impression you are treated to is that you should get the hell out of there before the building makes you dead, and that impression becomes a certainty when you see the fishbowl elevators whizzing up and down at the junctions of the walls like so many glass-enclosed coffins. It was doing my High Anxiety no good.

But I didn't cut and run. Instead I kept repeating to myself Professor Lillolman's exhortation to "Fight it! Fight it!" as Brophy and I checked in at the desk.

"Dr. Thorndyke, you're all set," said the desk clerk. "You and Mr. Brophy are in 1702 and 1703."

I felt the sweat breaking out on me. *Seventeen!* "Excuse me," I said, "I thought that I had specifically requested a room on a lower floor. Nothing higher than three."

"Well, we had 201 all ready for you," the desk clerk said. "However a Mr. MacGuffin called this morning and had us change it to the seventeenth floor."

"MacGuffin?" I said. "MacGuffin? I don't know anyone by that name."

"Isn't that strange," said Brophy. "Isn't that strange."

"I'm sorry, sir," said the desk clerk. "We can't do anything about it now. We're all booked up. But maybe we can make a change tomorrow."

"Aw, c'mon, Doc," Brophy chimed in. "It's only for a coupla nights."

It was clear that my sidekick found this deathtrap a fascinating place, and there was still Lillolman's voice in my head, saying, "Fight it! Fight it!" So I gave in. "I guess it'll be all right," I said, knowing for a cold hard fact that it wouldn't be.

A bellboy appeared, picked up our keys, and took charge of our bags. "Is there anything I can get you, sir?" he asked.

"Yes. I'd like a newspaper," I answered. I was extremely anxious to see if there had been any further news about Wentworth's demise.

"Gotcha," said the bellboy, with that mindless tone of Keystone Cops efficiency that virtually guarantees an eventual failure to deliver the goods. "I'll get you one and meet you at the elevators."

"Please don't forget," I said in a futile effort to fend off the inevitable. "It's very important."

He gave me that terrible look that bellboys have developed, halfway between blank incomprehension and overt hostility. "Yeah, all right. Okay," he said churlishly, the overt hostility having apparently gotten the upper hand.

Brophy and I walked slowly to the elevators, I repeating "Fight it!" to myself with each step and Brophy gazing enraptured at the walls of doom looming over us. "Wow," he said, "talk about modern."

The bellboy met us at the elevator and graciously gestured us inside.

Fight it Fight it Fight it Fight it Fight it Fight it Fight it Fight it.

"Here we go," said the bellboy. "All the way to the top."

Fight it Fi——"Wait!" I blurted. "I'll walk."

But it was too late.

"What?" said Brophy and the bellboy in unison.

"Nothing," I replied. Nothing but terror.

One thing I will say for that elevator: it was fast. I was only on my fourteenth Fight it! of the upward journey when the bellboy jolted me out of my concentration with, "Quite a view, isn't it?"

I hadn't really focused on it till then, but all at once the true nature of my situation was brought home to me, and in a quiet manful way I started to whimper and jibber incoherently.

At last the elevator came to a soul-wrenching halt. "Here we are," said the bellboy. "Top floor. Top of the hotel. You can't get any higher. Watch your step. We're way up there. We're pretty high."

With very little effort this lad was fully capable of getting on my nerves. "All right, already," I shouted. "We know we're high."

"Seventeen," he said in a chastened voice, and as the doors opened, "This way please."

We followed him out of the elevator and along the corridor, one side of which was a nice solid wall punctuated by nice solid doors and the other side of which was an eensie little railing and a nice big empty reaching-out ravenous void. "Wow!" Brophy chirped. "Hey Doc, look at this. What a view! This is spectacular!"

I moved closer to the nice solid wall. Fight it Fight it Fight it. "I can see it from here," I said. "It's very nice. Very nice."

Suddenly from out of one of the nice solid doors came a nice solid supply cart pushed by a nice solid male attendant. It hit me blindside and sent me reeling toward that eensie little railing. *"Ohhhhhhhhh . . ."* it occurred to me to say. High Anxiety struck like a truncheon—and there was no fighting it. All the symptoms came crashing down on me at once: nausea, blurred vision, dizziness. My hands clawed the air. My feet kicked and fought for some sort of hold on the corridor floor. I felt my body tipping slowly but unmistakably into the void. *"Aaauuuuggghhhh!"*

I was more than halfway over when I felt Brophy's arms grab me around the waist. I remember praying that I wouldn't hear him shout, "I got it! I got it! I got it!" for then we both were doomed. But he exerted all his strength and just barely managed to pull me back from the brink. If possible, he was more terrified than I was, and for some reason his anxiety seemed to calm me down.

"Are you all right, Doc?" he asked frantically. "Are you all right?"

"I'm all right. I'm all right," I said. "Thank you, Brophy. Thank you."

That habit of his of saying everything twice was beginning to get out of hand.

"Sorry," said the nice solid male attendant in an irritated voice. "I didn't know anybody was there." And with that curt apology he wheeled his cart off down the corridor, obviously secure in the belief that only a congenital idiot would be stupid enough to walk a hotel corridor without honking.

"Boy," said Brophy, "if you would have gone over you would have been smashed like corned beef hash. Your brains would have spattered all over the lobby. Your guts—"

"Brophy! *Please!*" I said, and he subsided.

"1702," said the bellboy, opening the door. He placed my suitcase on the luggage stand, opened the drapes, adjusted the air conditioning, and performed all those other useless services designed to increase a tip. But had he performed the service I had asked him to perform? That was the question.

"Is there anything else I can do for you?" he inquired, obviously proud of his exertions.

"No," I answered, handing him a dollar and dreading what was sure to come next. "Where's my newspaper, by the way?"

"Oh, the newstand didn't have any left, and I didn't want to go around the corner."

I noted that the explanation for "didn't" was "didn't want to," and I said with some emphasis, "It — is — important — that — I — get — that — newspaper."

"All right. All right. I'll get you the paper. I'll get you the paper."

The Brophy double-talk disease was spreading.

The bellboy went next door to get my sidekick established. I began to unpack, being careful to leave my door wide open. Thus I was able to see the bellboy passing on his way back to the elevator, and I called out to him, "Don't forget that paper."

That, apparently, was the next-to-last straw as far as he was concerned.

"*All right!* I'll get it! I'll get it! What's so important about a lousy stinking newspaper?"

I treated that as a rhetorical question, and when he was out of sight I called down to the desk and asked them to remind him gently not to forget.

After all the sweating I'd done in the previous thirty minutes, I now badly wanted and needed a shower. I hastily completed my unpacking, stripped off my wrinkled suit and soggy shirt, slipped on my terry cloth robe, and headed for the heavenly therapy of clean-scented soap and streaming warm water. The pressure in the shower was luxuriously strong. I adjusted the temperature of the pelting spray, testing it with my hand, and I sensed my muscles begin to unknot as the bathroom filled with billows of steamy fog. Finally the temperature was where I liked it. I got out of my robe and stepped into the shower, pulling the curtain across behind me. It seemed, for the few seconds of peace that were granted me, that I had left all my earthly troubles behind, far far away on the other side of that sheet of transluscent plastic.

There is an old Russian proverb that says, "You are never in greater danger than when you feel most safe." I could not have felt much safer than I did in that shower. Of course, it should have long since become clear to me that the strange occurrences and unanswered questions of the previous few days demanded an attitude of constant caution and vigilance on my part. Even a little paranoia wouldn't have hurt. But I was terribly slow to learn the lesson, so as I luxuriated in the warmth of the falling water I did not notice through the shower curtain that there was a figure framed in my bathroom doorway. I did not notice that the figure was gripping something in its right hand, something long and silver-gray in color.

There was the sudden shock as the curtain was ripped off the rings, the micro-second's vision of a pair of maddened eyes, the helpless horror as the raised right arm descended.

"Here!" screamed the bellboy, stabbing me in the chest. *"Here!"* he screamed again thrusting at my throat. *"Here!"* A vicious jab in my stomach. *"Here!"* A painful jolt into my ribs.

"Here's your paper! Here's your paper! Here's your paper!"

And there, indeed, it was, the *San Francisco Examiner*, getting thoroughly wet.

"Here's your lousy stinking paper!" the bellboy was screeching. "Happy now? Happy now? Happy now? Happy now?"

The *Examiner* was too soggy to poke me with anymore, so after one final squish in my abdomen the bellboy flung the paper down and stalked out.

I watched him as he left. I sat there at the bottom of the tub, the water beating on my head, and mumbled, "What a nervous kid!"

CHAPTER VIII

The next morning, about half an hour before I was scheduled to give my speech, I was in my room reading over the text one final time. I had almost finished when there was a knock on the door.

By then I had begun at last to exercise a little caution. Tiptoeing silently to the door, I said in a soft voice, "Who is it? It's not the bellboy, is it?" Slowly and carefully I opened the door a tiny little crack.

CRASH! It flew open, and a perfectly stunning creature with blonde hair and cupid's-bow lips rushed into the room. She was elegantly dressed in a fashionable gray suit. Beneath her big picture hat her devastating chestnut-brown eyes flashed out a messsge of fear and desperation. She pressed her back against the wall and darted nervous glances around the room as the door slammed shut.

"Who are—"I began to ask.

"Get away from the door," she said in a hoarse whisper, her right hand plunging into her purse and grasping hold of something, something that could only be a gun.

"Just a second, Miss—" I said as a bolt of fear ran through my insides.

"Get away from me," she snapped. "Don't move. Be quiet. They'll hear you. Close the drapes."

It occurred to me that I was dealing with a beautiful victim of paranoia—a beautiful *armed* victim—so I went to do as she'd asked.

"Get down!" she said vehemently. "They'll see you."

Paranoid. Definitely. I crouched down and closed the drapes.

"Close the other one," she commanded.

Paranoid and pushy. I obediently started across the room.

"Keep down," she ordered.

She was so obviously scared and so much more obviously pretty that I really didn't mind being bossed around by her. Her gun impressed me too. I got back in my crouch as she had commanded.

"Come here," she said after I'd closed the drapes.

Still in a crouch, I started across the room toward her.

"Get up," she said.

I rose and continued approaching.

"Sit down," she said.

I started to sit.

"Not there," she said.

"Where?" I said.

"Here," she replied, pointing to the bed.

"Here?" I asked.

"There," she answered.

I sat, but immediately sensed the pressure of a full bladder. I got up to go to the bathroom.

"Don't go," she said.

"Please," I lied, "you made me very nervous. I have to go."

"Then don't flush," she begged. "They'll hear you."

Say, this girl was serious. "I don't have to go that badly," I said, then walked back to the bed and sat down. "Now, who are you and who are 'they'?"

"Don't ask," she snapped, but right away she softened. "Don't ask. I know I'm being followed."

Suddenly there was the sound of the doorknob turning. Damn! I hadn't relocked the door. "Quick," she said. "Make believe you know me." And with that she pulled me to her and kissed me as no paranoid had ever kissed me before.

Fortunately, it was just the maid. "Sorry," she said wrinkling her nose in disgust. "I'll come back later."

She left all too quickly, in that, as soon as she left, the mysterious lady stopped kissing me. "What's your sign?"

She looked at me coldly. "I'm sorry, it's unlisted."

"Who are you?" I asked.

"My name is Victoria Brisbane. My father is Arthur Brisbane."

I could hardly believe it. "You're the cocker's daughter?"

Somehow that didn't sound right.

But she took no notice. "Have you seen my father at the Institute? Is he all right?"

How could I answer that question? The secret Code of Sound Medical Practice specifically forbids telling a patient's immediate family the truth about his condition. So I said, "Oh . . . uh . . . he's fine. He's coming along fine. He's very affectionate. He licked me."

"He what?"

Drat! I had let the dog out of the bag. "Well," I admitted, "you know he thinks he's a dog these days."

"A dog? Dr. Thorndyke, my father is as sane as I am."

All I said was, "Hmmmmm."

"Dr. Thorndyke," Miss Brisbane said, her fabulous chestnut eyes sparkling, "eighteen months ago my father had a nervous breakdown. He went into the Institute for a rest and has been a virtual prisoner there ever since. Frankly, Doctor, I fear for his life."

Her voice vibrated with daughterly love and deep human anguish. Then too, there was something in her words that seemed to fit in with the odd goings-on at the Institute. Something, but how much?

Victoria Brisbane (Madeline Kahn) enters Thorndyke's hotel room.

I said, "Miss Brisbane, I assure you, I am a competent psychiatrist. I've met your father and I must tell you, in my professional capacity, that he is deeply disturbed."

An unexpected knock on the door caused me to be deeply disturbed myself for a moment. Paranoia is catching.

"Don't answer it," whispered Miss Brisbane. "If they know I'm here with you, they'll harm my father."

What a relief it was to hear Brophy's familiar voice, although I can't imagine what else I was expecting. "Hey, Doc." he called. "You're late. They're expecting you at the convention hall."

"I'll be right down," I shouted, and turning to Miss Brisbane I said, "It's all right. That's Brophy, my driver. Please excuse me. I must go. They're waiting for me."

A cloud of desperation, almost grief, came over her face. "Don't you believe me?" she moaned. "Don't you believe what I'm telling you?"

I didn't really, but I knew I really wanted to. "Listen," I said, "I've got to go to the convention now. Why don't we meet downstairs at the bar later. We'll talk about it."

That seemed to lift her spirits. "Later at the bar. Good."

I hurried put together my speech manuscript and some other materials and accompanied Miss Brisbane out the door. She sure was neat looking! As we walked down the corridor I tried to calm her fears a bit, keeping one eye peeled at all times for supply carts. "See?" I said. "Nobody's here. There are no enemies. There's nothing to worry about."

I actually believed what I was saying, but if I'd been looking around for bad guys instead of supply carts I would have noticed immediately that each of the three statements I'd just made was false, and that the last one was the falsest of them all.

Victoria Brisbane was a non-Jewish-American princess, or a Jewish-American princess who happened to be a WASP. In other words, she suffered—if "suffered" is the word—from the syndrome of endless paternal pampering and consequent father fixation. In other words, she and her father were innocently and unconsciously stuck on each other.

Born into the cream of San Francisco society in 1950, Vicki Brisbane knew only luxury and refinement from her earliest years. Her mother, Doris Wilber Brisbane, was from an old Peninsula family and was famous before and after her marriage for a classic beauty that many said was purer than Gene Tierney's, more striking than Joan Fontaine's. Doris Brisbane was also, however, at best a reluctant mother. Social pressure and a sense of duty more than any urge of maternal instinct had motivated Doris to submit to impregnation,

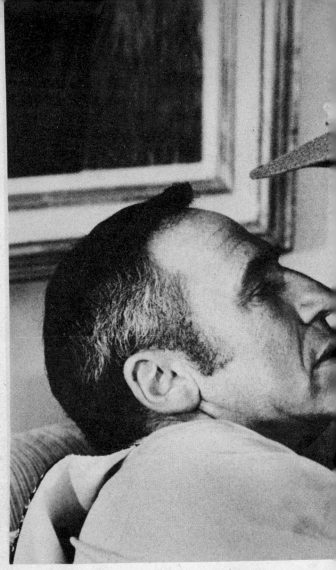
Thorndyke and Brisbane contact each other.

and once the tedium of pregnancy and the discomforts of childbirth were done with she felt that she had done her bit. The care and nurturing of her daughter, therefore, were delegated to nurses, governesses, teachers, and butlers while Doris returned to the social whirl from which she had been excluded by a child-swollen womb.

The emotional void thus created was filled imperfectly but lovingly—by Doris' husband, Arthur Brisbane. As the head of Brisbane Industries, Vicki's father was far too busy to devote a great amount of time to his only child, but what time he had was hers unreservedly. Nothing she *might* have wanted ever went unbought. Wherever they went, whatever they did, Arthur Brisbane and his daughter were an idyllic pair.

As Vicki grew older her relationship with her father deepened. As she passed through the primary and secondary grades of girls' schools in and around San Francisco she began to value her devoted parent not just as a father, but as a counselor, a mentor, a friend. Then, just before Vicki's nineteenth birthday, Doris Brisbane died in the crash of a Boeing 707 which crashed into a mountainside while attempting an emergency landing at Wheeling, West Virginia.

This sudden common loss wedded Vicki and her father an even tighter union than before. They sought to comfort one another in their bereavement, and even took a certain dimly perceived pleasure in the realization that now each was all the other had left in the world—apart from several dozen million dollars.

Vicki had been at school in the small village of Les Avants above Lake Geneva in Switzerland when word of her mother's death was brought to her. She immediately returned to San Francisco, and after the funeral and period of mourning stayed on to fill her mother's shoes in the capacity of her father's hostess and lady of the house. In this role she watched with increasing anxiety as Arthur Brisbane's grief and advancing years combined with a steady diet of overwork served to place him under an intolerable strain. Late in 1975 he had a nervous breakdown and Vicki, seeking the best professional advice, was advised to commit him to The Psycho-Neurotic Institute For The Very, *Very* Nervous. One of her advisers, the Brisbane family doctor, also made the affectionate suggestion that Vicki now devote a little less time to her father and a little more time to putting together a family of her own. She had received such advice many times before, and knew that it was easier to give than to follow. For her desire of a family was contingent on finding a suitable mate, and "suitable" meant someone as wonderful as her incomparable father.

As Thorndyke and Miss Brisbane walk down the corridor a sinister figure watches them from the shadows across the courtyard. He's wearing a tight-

fitting black suit and black leather gloves. A livid scar runs along his cheek, and his eyes are the cold dead eyes of a killer. As his gaze follows the Doctor and the young woman into an elevator his lips part in an ugly and threatening smile. Sets of multiple braces cover his teeth to such an extent that one can barely see the white enamel. From a distance one might think that his mouth was filled with steel.

He watches the elevator descend and then walks to a nearby pay phone. He places a call. A voice can be heard answering. He mutters a few words. The voice responds.

"*I don't know what they said,*" *he whispers.* "*All I know is that they met. What do you want me to do? Kill him? If you want me to kill him, I'll kill him. I don't have to kill him, but I'd like to kill him. I killed Ashley. I helped kill Wentworth. Another killing or two won't make any difference. It would make me happy. I'd like to kill them both. I think it would be better if I killed them both.*

The voice on the phone replies.

"*Well, let me kill just one then,*" *the man with the braces pleads.* "*Whichever one you want.*"

The voice on the phone is heard again.

"*All right,*" *says the killer.* "*I'll wait. But the minute you say kill them, I'll kill them. I'll kill them both. I'd love to kill them. I'm dying to kill them.*"

He listens for a second or two, then hangs up. As he

*walks toward the elevator there is a smile on his face.
His braces glitter. Clearly he is a man who is looking
forward to something with a degree of eager anticipation that is almost obscene.*

CHAPTER IX

I gave my speech on "Some Aspects of Psycho-Biological Therapy" to an audience of about a hundred of my colleagues in one of the hotel's meeting rooms. It was good to see so many old friends and co-workers in the rows of chairs in front of the dais, and it was tremendously satisfying to have hanging behind me as I spoke large photographs of the great pioneers of our profession: Dr. Sigmund Freud, Dr. Otto Rank, Dr. Karl Jung, Dr. Alfred Alder, Dr. Joyce Brothers.

My address was well received, and when I'd finished I threw the floor open to questions. The first man to raise his hand was an eminent Post-Jungian-Gestalt-Primal-Scream-Therapist. "Dr. Thorndyke," he said, "you mentioned in your talk that penis envy should be deemed an outmoded psychiatric concept. Could you expand on that?"

I could indeed. "Let's remember," I said, "that the term penis envy was created in a predominantly male atmosphere of. . . ."

I trailed off because a well-respected Neo-Freudian-Transactional-Encounter-Group therapist had entered the meeting room with his two daughters, age ten and twelve. "I'm sorry I'm late," he said. "Forgive me for bringing the kids. I couldn't find a sitter."

I gave him a friendly nod and continued. "As I was saying, in a world of predominantly male-orientated psychology it was only natural to arrive at the term pe——"

But I noticed those four innocent young eyes looking up at me.

"Pee-pee envy," I concluded.

Fortunately, the eminent analyst Dr. Isaiah Gottfried, who now raised his hand, was as alert as I was to the dangers of polluting unformed minds with references to the more delicate portions of the human anatomy. He asked, "Are you saying there is absolutely no validity to . . . pee-pee envy?"

I heaved a sigh of relief. We had avoided a terrible danger. "It has no more validity," I replied, "than if we said a man envied a woman's. . . ." (Uh-oh! It seemed that the terrible danger had to be avoided some more. A quick glance in the direction of the two girls had stopped me just in the nick of time.) ". . . a woman's *balloons*," I concluded.

A former colleague of mine from Harvard rose and asked, "Dr. Thorndyke, do you feel that the trauma of toilet training has a bearing on the future sexuality of the adolescent?"

We were treading on thin ice again. "Toilet training is a vast area," I said. "Are we talking about number one or cocky-doody?"

"Well, for the sake of argument," came the answer, "let's say cocky-doody."

"Cocky-doody, good. In my professional opinion, I would have to say that going potty has very little to do with future sexual development. Let me backtrack for a second. The female erogenous zone—"

"You mean the balloons?" Dr. Gottfried asked.

Oh dear!

"No, no, no," I replied. "Lower. Lower. Much lower. Where the babies come out. The wo . . . The woo-woo."

"The woo-woo?"

"Yes! The woo-woo! One of the most important feminine organs known to man!"

This declaration resulted in thunderous applause, and in a general agreement that the question period should be brought to a close, fast.

Convention activities took up the rest of the day, so I met Miss Brisbane in the bar shortly before dinner time. It was a pleasant place, softly lighted and relaxed in mood. There was a large black piano in the center of the room, and a bass player, a drummer, and the pianist provided a gentle rhythmic background for drinks and conversation. Miss Brisbane and I were seated in a comfortable booth near the musicians, who cast occasional admiring glances in our direction. I should say, in Miss Brisbane's direction. She was simply breathtaking in a stylish black evening gown that clung to the curves of her body with subtle yet provocative sensuality.

"Here we are," said the waitress, bringing our drinks. "A B & B, and a B & B & B."

As Miss Brisbane sipped from her glass, she peered in the dim light at my name tag. "Dr. Richard H. Thorndyke. What's the 'H' for?"

"What?" I said. In fact I had heard what she'd said, but I found the subject she'd raised so embarrassing that I pretended I hadn't.

"The 'H'," she repeated. "Your middle initial. What does it stand for?"

"Harpsbo," I mumbled, speaking as indistinctly as I could.

"What?" Miss Brisbane responded.

Oh the hell with it. "Harpo!" I said loudly.

"Harpo?" she repeated in disbelief.

"My mother loved the Marx Brothers," I hastened to explain. "She saw all their movies. She named me Harpo."

Miss Brisbane gave me a somewhat doubtful look, but then said, "Harpo. It's very nice. It suits you."

"Thank you," I said, hoping that the subject could now be dropped.

It could be and was. We turned our attention to the question of Arthur Brisbane and his treatment at the Institute.

Having had a chance to think it over during the day, I had come to the conclusion that the best way to convince Miss Brisbane of her father's condition was to let her see it for herself. I didn't know how she would react to the idea, so I led up to it gradually. When I finally did make the suggestion, it came as an immense relief to both of us to learn that she had been planning to make the exact same proposal herself. We had a good laugh and raised our glasses into the air. "To Daddy's recovery," she said, and we clinked and drank.

"Feeling better?" I asked her.

"Oh Dr. Thorndyke, you'll never know how happy it makes me to think I'll soon be able to visit my father at the Institute."

"I must warn you, Miss Brisbane," I said. "I think you're going to be in for quite a shock."

"I don't care," she responded bravely. "I know if I can see him and talk to him everything will be all right."

All at once, without either of us knowing how, we found ourselves looking deeply into each other's eyes. For a brief moment of time the world disappeared, and there was only us.

We both noticed the silence at the same time.

"Would you excuse me," Miss Brisbane said, flushing a little. "I'll be right back. I've got to go to the little girls' room."

I slid out of the booth to let her pass, but in doing so I inadvertently knocked her purse off the table. The contents spilled out on the floor. "I'm so sorry," I said, and started picking up the various objects scattered about. Her wallet was among them, and as I put it on the table I noticed a picture inside of Victoria and an older man. "Forgive me for prying," I said, pointing to the photo, "but who is this gentleman?"

Whether it was some sixth sense that prompted me to ask or only simply jealousy, the answer I got shook me to the ground. Apparently surprised that I hadn't recognized the man, Miss Brisbane replied, "Why, that's Daddy."

"Daddy?" I said. "Are you trying to tell me that this man is Arthur Brisbane, your father?"

"Of course."

Suddenly it became clear to me that this young lady and I were involved in something extremely sinister. "This is not the man I examined at the Institute," I said. "Something is very *very* wrong."

I was very *very* right about that, and I would have realized just how right if I had noticed that watching us just one booth away was a black-gloved black-suited man with a massively complex set of children's braces on his teeth.

Dr. Montague and Nurse Diesel are seated sipping coffee in the latter's office. Montague appears nervous, almost distraught, and even Nurse Diesel is showing signs of worry.

"What are we going to do?" *says Montague anxiously.* "This is serious. He knows. He's seen the picture. He knows that's not the real Brisbane we showed him. What'll we do? What'll we do? We'll have to kill him. We'll have to let him kill him."

Nurse Diesel silences him with a sneer of contempt. "That's all we need now, another killing. First Ashley, then Wentworth. We can't kill Thorndyke without the police suspecting something."

Montague's voice rises to a panicky pitch. "But what are we going to do? What if he goes to the police?"

Nurse Diesel smiles coldly. "I've thought of that. He won't *go to the police if he* can't *go to the police.*"

"I don't understand," *says Montague.* "What do you mean if he can't *go to the police? Why can't he go to the police?*"

"Because the police will be after *him.*"

"Why will the police be after *him?*"

"Because Doctor Richard H. Thorndyke is going to kill somebody."

CHAPTER X

I of course was unaware of the grisly fact that I was shortly going to take someone's life, and I spent the evening getting as much information as possible from Victoria about her father and his treatment at the Institute. I personally escorted her back to her apartment, kissed her lightly on the lips—I didn't trust myself with anything more passionate—and waited outside until I heard her bolt and latch her door. It was a relief to know that she was safe, for the moment at least.

Back at the hotel I debated with myself as to whether I should telephone the police. What could I tell them? That my colleagues at the Institute had shown me one patient when I had asked to see another? That certainly wasn't a crime. That Arthur Brisbane was being kept a prisoner at the Institute? That was sheer speculation. And even granting that Brisbane was not a cocker

117

spaniel, that still didn't rule out the possibility that he was seriously disturbed in some other way. I had the Institute's reputation to think of. I couldn't unloose a scandal just because there were some unanswered questions floating in the air. No, I decided, the best thing to do was to head back to the Institute first thing in the morning and find out for myself exactly what was going on.

I roused Brophy at seven A.M. and told him to get us packed and checked out as quickly as possible. He was heartbroken because he hadn't yet had a chance to take any pictures of the hotel's spectacular lobby. I said he would have plenty of time to take pictures if he got our luggage ready and our bill paid before I finished dressing. That was all the incentive he needed.

He left for the lobby around seven-fifteen, and about five minutes later a bellboy arrived to collect our bags.

"Good morning, Dr. Thorndyke," he said cheerfully. "Would you like a copy of this morning's paper?"

"*No!*" I shouted scaring the poor man half to death. Not all bellboys were evil, I had to remind myself, as I said to him, "I beg your pardon. I mean, no thank you. I already read the paper yesterday. I mean, no news is good news."

He gave me a wary look as he picked up the suitcases. "Bunch o' nuts at this shrink convention," I heard him mutter under his breath.

The elevator trip to the lobby was average terrifying, but I didn't mind it so much because I knew that this was the last such ride I would have to take. Nothing prepared me for what was going to happen when I got to the ground floor.

The doors opened and I stepped out. Directly in front of me I saw . . . "me"! Except *this* "me" had a smoking .38-caliber revolver in his black-gloved hand. We stood staring at each other for two or three seconds. Then he stripped off the mask he was wearing and revealed a hideous metal-encrusted smile. The smile broadened as he pushed the gun into my midsection butt first. Still smiling, he turned and walked away.

Bewildered and bemused, I walked in the direction of the desk while examining the revolver I now held in my hand. Everything around me seemed to be going on in slow motion. I felt strangely disembodied and utterly disoriented. Why in heaven's name was some strange man wearing my face? Some strange man with a smoking .38 in his hand, to be precise. Why was Brophy taking pictures of the lobby's floor—or was it something lying on the lobby's floor? Why was everyone staring at me with expressions of horror in their eyes? Why was that woman pointing in my direction and screaming, "That's him! There he is!"

Seeing me approaching, Brophy ran up to me, camera in hand. "Doc! Doc! Why did you do it? Why did you do it?"

"Do what? Do what?" I said in a daze.

Thorndyke ostensibly goes berserk and kills a fellow
psychiatrist.

The real killer rips off his rubber "Thorndyke" mask in triumph.

"Shoot that man there," he replied, pointing down at the inert body of a psychiatrist I'd been friendly with for several years, a psychiatrist who now had one bullet wound in the middle of his forehead and two bullet wounds in the middle of his chest.

My God! I thought. How can this be happening?

There was Brophy, his face contorted in anguish and confusion. There was the woman who had screamed, gesturing frantically in my direction. There was a man pointing at me and shouting, "Get him!" There was another man shouting, "Call the police!" There was a security guard reaching for the gun in his holster while another security guard moved cautiously toward where I was standing.

All this must be happening to someone else, I thought. The whole world can't have gone mad in the space of thirty seconds.

Then, in a sudden violent flash, everything came together in my mind: the mask, the gun, the body, the blood.

Sweet God in heaven! Someone with my face had committed murder!

The security guards were inching toward me. I could hear police sirens from outside. "Wait!" I yelled. "You don't understand! There was another man! I didn't . . . It wasn't me. . . ."

The eyes and the faces bearing down on me didn't look ready to listen. They kept on coming. Stark terror gripped my mind. I had to escape! I waved the gun menacingly and started to back away. I could see policemen racing toward the lobby door. Over my shoulder I caught sight of a red "Exit" sign. Praying that no one would start shooting at me in a crowded hotel lobby, I turned my back and ran for my life.

Dressed in her robe, Nurse Diesel is lying on her bed. In her hands she holds a newspaper, and on the newspaper's front page is a picture of "Dr. Thorndyke" in the act of shooting a colleague. Above the picture is the banner headline: PSYCHIATRIST GOES BESERK.

Nurse Diesel is plainly delighted with what she sees. She laughs gleefully and says, "It's all working. It's all working exactly as I planned. Soon Thorndyke will be out of our way forever."

She laughs again. It is not a pleasant sound.

From above her Dr. Montague sings her praises. "You're brilliant. You're evil. But you're brilliant."

He is suspended from a giant pulley on the ceiling, his arms and legs spread wide. He is dressed like a Roman slave in leather rags.

"Thank you," says Nurse Diesel smugly, flicking a small whip at Montague's thighs. "Now, should our esteemed patient, Mr. Arthur Brisbane, in a fit of extreme depression, decide to take his own life. . . ."

Montague winces in ecstasy as the whip bites at his skin. "Oh, I love your mind," he says. "Is the Brisbane estate insurance policy made out to the Institute?"

"Of course, you putz," Nurse Diesel spits. "Do you

think I'm an amateur? And signed I might add. Just think of it. One hundred and eighty million dollars." She hugs herself lovingly. *"Ohhh. This is a great day."*

"More whip!" pleads Montague.

Nurse Diesel ignores him. "I feel so good," she says, "that I'm going to do something I haven't done in years. I'm . . . going . . . to . . . let . . . my . . . hair . . . down."

Montague's eyes widen with extravagant lust. Plainly the whip no longer interests him. "Oooohhh," he squeals. "You've promised, but you've never done it."

"I'm going to do it," says Nurse Diesel, wetting her lips.

"Yes! Yes!" Montague roars. "Do it! Do it!"

Nurse Diesel rises from her bed. Slowly, sensuously, she removes one bobby pin after another, and great waterfalls of hair cascade down to the ground all around her. Then, suggestively twisting her body, she removes her robe. A silky diaphanous floor-length skirt clings to her hips. Her stomach is bare. Her breasts are cupped in golden carvings of sharp-fanged snakes that curl around her flesh to form a sort of brassiere. She returns to the bed and reclines, looking up at Montague slavering above her.

"Okay," she snaps, arranging her long hair around her. "I'm ready."

She pulls a golden tassel near her bed and a motor

starts to hum. Montague begins a slow descent toward her waiting body.

"I love you, Cleopatra, I love you!" he cries as the vision of Nurse Diesel comes nearer and nearer.

Excited now and breathing heavily herself, Nurse Diesel gasps out, "Go, Spartacus, go!"

Clearly, these are two people who are celebrating, who feel that everything is going their way, that no one can stop them, that some ultimate victory is finally within their grasp.

CHAPTER XI

While Diesel and Montague were playing out their tender love scene at the Institute, I was standing in the shadows near Fisherman's Wharf waiting for Victoria Brisbane. I had spent the day scurrying around San Francisco in an effort to stay out of the clutches of the police. After escaping from the hotel I had hailed a cab and gone to Golden Gate Park. There I realized that I would be safer in a movie theater. So, after grabbing something to eat at a hot dog stand, I spent the afternoon in the back row of the West Bridge Cinema watching some silly cowboy-and-Indian shoot-'em-up three times through. Halfway through the second showing it had occurred to me to call Victoria. I hadn't tried to explain everything over the phone, just the most important details. I had asked her to trust me, and to meet me after dark near the Wharf. She had said she would come.

Now, as I waited for her, I went over once more in my mind the conclusions I had come to. Diesel and Montague had a hired killer working for them, a hired killer who was probably responsible for the deaths of both Ashley and Wentworth. Instead of having *me* killed, however, they had had me framed, presumably to keep suspicion from focusing on themselves. The one thing that Ashley, Wentworth, and I had in common was access to the inner workings of the Institute, and what those inner workings were was now fairly clear. Diesel and Montague were victimizing our wealthiest patients in order to get their money. True, that was a time-honored tradition in the psychiatric profession, but they were overdoing it.

I felt certain that Brophy was not involved with them. His face this morning when he had come running up to me was eloquent proof of his innocence. And as for that poor psychiatrist full of holes in the hotel lobby, well, he was dead proof of how unwise it is to be in the wrong place at the wrong time.

A long sleek automobile with the Louis Vuitton monogram embellishing its entire chassis pulled up at the curb a few yards from where I was waiting. I could see Victoria behind the wheel—immaculate, elegant, queenly in her bearing. Looking at her then I realized for the first time just how wealthy the Brisbane family was.

Then she saw me, and she jumped out of the car.

"Dr. Thorndyke! Dr. Thorndyke!" she called. "Richard! Richard!"

Then she was in my arms, and I held her.

After a long while she pulled back a little and looked into my eyes. "Oh, my darling. I'm so glad to see you. The world's gone mad. Nothing makes sense any more. I don't know what to believe or not to believe. My life is all topsy-turvy. One moment you're taking me home and protecting me and the next moment you're pumping bullets into an innocent man and then it's not you. It's the other Thorndyke. How much more can a girl take? I don't know where I am. I don't know who I am. I don't know what's happening anymore. . . ."

I pulled her to me. We held each other close. After a few minutes I sensed she was calmer, and I leaned back to look at her beautiful face.

". . . so worried about my father. I don't know where, who, what . . ."

I pulled her to me again and counted to fifty before letting go.

". . . nerves are cracking. I think I'm going to die. I feel like I'm going to explode. . . ."

I pulled her to me a third time. Obviously strong measures were in order. "All right, all right!" I said sternly. "That's enough, Vicki! That's enough!"

That stopped her. She looked up at me with those big chestnut eyes, lovely and apologetic. "I'm sorry," she said. "Please forgive me. I'm so close to my menstrual cycle I could scream."

A hell of a note. But I said, "Come on, we've got to

Thorndyke and Victoria begin to unravel the intricate plot.

think. My only way out of this is to prove that it wasn't me who committed that murder.''

Victoria looked at me as though I'd just suffered some tragic personal loss. Her eyes made me cold with apprehension.

''But how *can* you prove it? she asked. ''Especially now.''

''What do you mean, 'especially now'?'' I demanded in a voice choked with fear.

By way of reply she reached into her purse, took out a newspaper clipping, and silently put it into my hand.

One look at it and my legs went weak. It was a front-page picture of ''me'' shooting the psychiatrist in the hotel lobby. ''How did they get this picture?'' I asked aloud. ''Who took this picture?'' Then I remembered Brophy! Brophy, of course. My ''buddy'' Brophy.

But wait a minute! The hotel elevator was visible in the picture,. Could it possibly be that. . . . Yes! There was a figure visible in the glass-enclosed elevator. The real me.

''Look,'' I said to Victoria, taking out my pen and circling that part of the photo. ''See this dot? It's probably me!''

''But the figure's so tiny,'' she said. ''It's unrecognizable.''

''I know, so we've got to contact Brophy. He's got the negative, and he's got to blow this up and prove that's me in the elevator.''

"But Brophy left for the Institute this morning, didn't he?" Victoria said despairingly. "He's probably back there by now."

Right then I caught sight of a mounted policeman heading toward us down the street. As fast as I could I grabbed Victoria and kissed her passionately, so that my face was hidden by hers. After the policeman had passed I let her go.

"Whew!" she gasped. "How can you suddenly get so excited at a time like this? Don't get me wrong. It's not that I don't find it titillating. It's just that—"

"We've got to separate," I cut in.

"Gee you're fickle," she pouted.

"It's too dangerous," I explained. "We can't be seen together. I'll call Brophy and get him to blow up that picture. I'll call you tomorrow morning."

"But where will you sleep tonight?"

"I'll find some cheap hotel in the skid row district. That should be safe. Then I'll call you first thing in the morning."

We looked into each other's eyes for a long time. "Good night," I said as we shared a fleeting kiss. Then I watched her drive away.

I put the call through to Brophy from a phone booth in a nearby bar.

"Hey, Doc!" he said. "Are you okay?"

"I'm fine, Brophy. Now listen; you remember those pictures you were taking this morning?"

"Do I! The wire services gave me big bucks for one of them." There was a pause, then a remorseful, "I hope it didn't cause you any trouble, Doc."

"No trouble at all, I said, exercising great self-control. "Look, Brophy, do you have the negative of that picture that the wire services bought?"

"Yeah, sure."

"Well, enlarge it as much as you can, will you? I think you'll see that the figure in the elevator is the real me."

"The *real* you? You mean the guy who murdered that shrink was a phony?"

"That's exactly what I mean. He was wearing a mask."

"Hey, that's great, Doc. I didn't know how comfortable I'd be driving a killer around."

"The negative, Brophy, the negative."

"I'll get right on it, Doc. Call me back in five minutes."

Four minutes and thirty seconds later I called back.

"What's the news, Brophy?"

"It's in the developer now, Doc. Yeah. Yeah. Yeah. It's coming! It's coming! Holy Toledo! You're right, Doc! There *is* a figure in the elevator."

I tried to stay cool. "I *know* there's a figure in the elevator, Brophy. But is it recognizable? Is it *me*?"

"Can't tell, Doc. I gotta keep enlarging this thing until we can clearly see the face. It'll take a while though. Can you call me back in about an hour?"

Forty-five minutes later I called back—and my blood froze. "I'm sorry," said a voice that sounded strangely like that of the half-mustached orderly, Norton, "Mr. Brophy is no longer associated with the Institute."

About the same time that Norton was speaking to me, Nurse Diesel was on the phone with her steel-toothed assassin. She had discovered that the proof of my innocence was hidden on the front page of every newspaper in California. Now, with Brophy safely locked up in the North Wing Violent Ward, she reasoned that I was the only person left in the world who knew that such proof existed.

That meant that I had to die.

CHAPTER XII

Early the next morning I stumbled bleary-eyed out of the dingy flea-infested hotel where I'd spent the night. My eyes itched and my muscles ached from too little sleep and too much anxiety. I walked down Market Street to clear my mind in the cool dawn air, and near the Ferry Building I went into a telephone booth to call Vicki.

I heard her phone ring once, two times. Just on the third ring a black-gloved fist crashed through the glass side of the booth, twisted the receiver out of my hand, and wrapped the cord around my neck, very very tightly. The fist let go of the receiver to get a better grip on the cord, and so when Vicky answered on the fourth ring the phone was dangling near my shoulder.

"Hello?" I heard her say, but I couldn't reply because sound can't exit if air can't enter.

Thorndyke rushes to call Victoria.

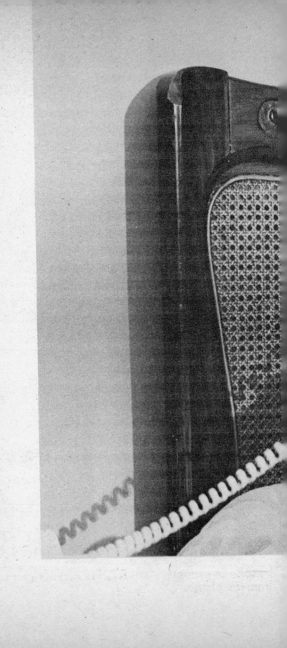

Victoria is puzzled at the strange sounds emanating from the phone.

"Hello?" she said again. I was struggling violently for breath, trying to escape the ever-tightening pressure round my throat. I heard myself making heavy wheezing sounds as I thrashed and kicked in a futile effort to get free. Vicki jumped to the wrong conclusion.

"Listen fella. I don't go for this kind of thing."

I managed to get one hand between my throat and the wire, but almost immediately the strangling pressure of the cord trapped it, and I could feel my wrist bone being forced into my Adam's apple. I gasped and huffed like a man with terminal asthma, which in a way was what I was.

"Who is this?" Victoria asked. "Listen, you're crazy if you think I'm going to stay on this phone and listen to heavy breathing."

It wasn't working. I was making a lot of noise, but no air was coming in. Red spots started dancing in front of my eyes.

"Listen," Victoria went on, "maybe other girls get turned on with these kinky phone calls, but I couldn't care less. How did you get my unlisted phone number? Did someone I know give it to you? . . . Listen, mister, I'm not going to listen to any more of this. I've had just about *enough!* . . . What are you wearing?"

It was horrible. I was being strangled to death while listening to the girl I loved mistake me for a pervert. It made me wild with terror and despair. It made me want to wail and sob. The only sound I could squeeze out, however, was a sort of squeaky, "Jeeeeee . . . Jeeeeee. . . ."

"Jeans?" said Victoria. "You're wearing jeans? I bet they're tight."

The red dots were turning into purple dots, and the morning sunlight seemed to be getting darker. Dear God! I was losing consciousness. I was beginning to die!

"Hello? Hello?" came Vicki's voice, a trace of irritation in it. "I can't hear you. You're starting to fade."

As I struggled, the back of my shoulder brushed up against a long glass shard that was hanging down from the point where the black fist had smashed through. I had brushed against it several times as I writhed around, but only now—perhaps too late—did I realize its potential value. With my free hand I reached spastically for my handkerchief. Everything was getting very dark now, and very hazy as the brain began to die from lack of oxygen. Finally I had the handkerchief in my hand, and with a last surge of strength I used it to get a firm grip on the dangling glass shard. I was close to blacking out now, but I managed to shift my body so I could reach around to the side of the booth. Unseeing, half-conscious, guided only by an animal instinct for survival, I thrust the glass dagger as hard as I could into flesh.

I was lucky. The shard sank in right between the killer's shoulder blades. Immediately the black glove released the cord, and from the ghastly steel-toothed mouth came a gruesome flow of rasping, gurgling, coughing sounds of death. The man sprawled against

"Braces" (Rudy DeLuca) strangles Thorndyke.

the booth, gasping and clawing at the air. Then, with one great spasm of shuddering breath, he sank to the ground, dead.

"You *animal!*" Victoria exclaimed, still not quite getting the point.

I stood there looking down at the body, rubbing my throat, revelling in the clear easy flow of oxygen to my lungs. The whole struggle couldn't have lasted much more than a minute, but the deserted streets and buildings of early dawn seemed to me almost like a brand new universe. After a few seconds of joy in being alive, I picked up the receiver. "Hello, Victoria? It's me, Richard."

"Richard? Richard?" she said. "Oh, I knew it was you all the time. I went along with it. Did you laugh? I laughed."

I paused for a moment. "Victoria, I've just killed a man."

"Another one? Richard, you've got to get a grip on yourself."

"No, you don't understand. I just killed the man who *really* killed the man in the lobby. Never mind. We have no time. Those fiends at the Institute know about the picture. They've got Brophy. They've got the negative. They've got everything."

Victoria's voice was anguished. "What are we going to do now? How can we prove you're innocent?"

"We've got to get back to the Institute," I said. "Our only hope now is to find your father and expose Montague and Diesel."

"How are we going to do that? The police are looking for you all over the city."

That was certainly a problem. "Victoria," I said, "go to the Salvation Army."

"Are they good at this sort of thing?"

"No! Just go to the Salvation Army and get some old clothes that you and I would never be caught dead in."

That sounded a little ambiguous on second thought.

"I mean, go to the Salvation Army and get some clothes for us that would have been fashionable in, say, Kiev, around 1947. If they can't get us to the Institute, nothing can."

It took us most of the day to get everything ready, but at nine o'clock that evening, with our lines rehearsed and our costumes in order, we arrived at San Francisco International Airport looking like the first-generation-East-European-immigrant version of Ma and Pa Kettle. We both carried shopping bags, and as a complement to Vicki's old-fashioned purse and rhinestone-encrusted eyeglasses, I was toting a cardboard carton bound up with twine. We had dusted some flour into our hair, and as we hobbled along arthritically in the direction of TWA Gate 26 a number of people favored us with that smug and superior smile that is the special bane of the aged and decrepit.

The ruse was working!

As we got near the gate I could see the sign, FLIGHT 201/LOS ANGELES, posted above the ramp entrance. It was time for us to go into our act.

"Here," said Vicki, right on cue, "put this celery in your bag. I can't carry no more."

Her accent was perfect: Molly Goldberg by way of Omsk.

"What the heck you buy celery in San Francisco for?" I grouched at her. "You can't get it at the market by the house? Celery I gotta schlepp."

"I thought in case we had a Bloody Mary on the plane."

"I don't like the Bloody Mary they give you. No sir. No sir. They put in too much Tabasco. It's too hot. Murray Weintraub—that's why he's dead today, from the Bloody Marys, from the hot, from the burning. It turned his stomach to a cinder."

"Not Murray Weintraub," Vicki interrupted. "Murray Weintraub is alive. He's making decals on shopping bags on Lincoln Road in Miami Beach. Oscar Birnbaum, he's dead from the Bloody Marys."

"No, no," I snapped back, "it's Murray."

We had now gotten to the baggage inspection station and the metal detectors. "Wait a minute," I said. "Wait a minute. What gate is this? I don't want to end up in Las Vegas. I can't take the excitement."

"Sir, said one of the security people, "would you please put your bags up here on this table."

I clutched my "luggage" to me. "Why do you want the bags? Why do you want the bags? Why can't I keep the bags?"

"We have to X-ray them."

"You want to X-ray the celery? What do you think we smuggled in the celery? The celery is for dip not for dope."

"Please, sir, there are others waiting."

That was true, I was happy to note, and their patience was beginning to wear thin. We were holding up progress at the metal detector.

"You go first," I said to Vicki.

She drew back. *"You* go first. I'm scared."

"Just go," I commanded.

She took a tentative step toward the metal detector and then stopped. "Just a second," she said to the attendant. "Is this a blower that blows up the skirt and gives everybody a free show?"

"God forbid!" I exclaimed, and Vicki went through.

"Sam, c'mon," she called from the other side. "Don't be afraid. It don't hurt."

This was my big moment, and I was enjoying our act so much I decided to ham things up a little. I turned to the crowd behind me and raised my arms like a man about to go over Niagara in a barrel. "All right, folks," I shouted. "Here I go!"

But when I turned back to the metal detector I saw Victoria on the far side staring at my midsection in horror.

The gun!

The gun the killer had handed me in the hotel lobby was plainly visible, jammed under my belt. I was

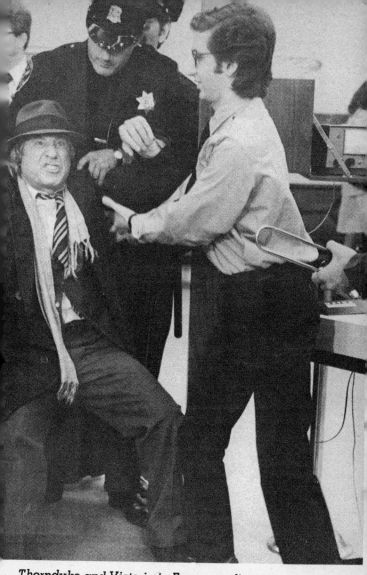

Thorndyke and Victoria in European disguise attempt to evade San Francisco airport authorities.

carrying it in case we needed it when we got to the Institute.

I quickly closed my jacket and smiled feebly at the guards. Fortunately they hadn't noticed anything.

But the metal detector would go crazy!

Ah well, it was too late to back out now. I would just have to bluff it through.

I went through, and the detector went "beep-beep."

"What's this? A game show?" I asked. "What do I win? A Pinto?"

"Sir, I'm afraid we'll have to search you, said the attendant.

Oh boy! I thought. Now for some real melodrama.

"Search me!" I cried aloud. "Search me! Take me. I'm a criminal. I'm a criminal. An old man beeped. Lock me up. Put me in prison. I beeped. I beeped."

At that point one of the policemen intervened and said to the attendant, "It's all right. Let him through." The attendant, alarmed by my bizarre behavior, was only too glad to agree. "It's all right, sir," he said, trying to calm me. "It's all right. You can go on."

Now for the grand finale, the frosting on the cake. "Thank you very much," I said with heavy dignity. "You're all nice boys. Write to your mother and father. Keep in touch. They don't forget so quick. They're people too."

The crowd backed up behind me was on the verge of becoming unruly, and the security people were getting frantic to be rid of me.

"They worry," I went on obliviously. "They wonder what's going on with you. Where you are and what you're doing. Children! They don't write. They don't care. You don't get a 'hello, pop.' You don't get nothing."

"Please *go!*" everyone was saying. They were practically ordering me to get on the plane and make my getaway.

They virtually shoved me toward the plane. Vicki and I were home free.

"You were wonderful," she whispered to me.

"You too," I replied.

"Now let's just hope it's a smooth flight. I hate it when it's bumpy."

Then, for the first time, it struck me: I was about to get into an airplane and *fly!*

Ah well, Vicki would have had to find out about my High Anxiety sometime. And I would try to be brave, for her.

CHAPTER XIII

The flight down to Los Angeles went smoothly. We rented a car at L.A. International and raced southward toward the Institute. I pulled off the road about a mile from the main gate. It was going on midnight. Vicki and I got rid of our disguises and climbed over the wall surrounding the Institute's grounds. From there it was only several hundred yards to the Administration Building.

We approached from the rear and made our way around to the side where Professor Lillolman's office was located. The lights were on, which indicated that he might just be there. We climbed in through an open window and tiptoed slowly toward the Professor's consulting room. He *was* there, seated in his swivel chair with his back toward us and his head tilted to one side. He was very still.

Lillolman appears to be dead.

For a moment I thought I might faint. If they had done something to Lillolman I wouldn't bother about exposing them. I'd just start shooting.

"Professor Lillo—" I started to say, but my throat was too dry to get the words out. I swallowed and tried again, "Professor Lillolman?"

I reached out to touch his arm, and every second the conviction grew in me that my dear old teacher had been killed.

"Professor?" I repeated, my voice quavering.

My hand came to rest on his slumping shoulder. He did not respond. A little pressure started his body and the swivel chair turning, and as Lillolman's face came into view I gazed with horror upon the unspeakable truth. With his tongue hanging loose from his mouth and his eyes staring blankly into space, his expression was terrible to behold.

"Oh my God!" Victoria shrieked. "He's dead!"

Lillolman bounded up out of his chair like a bantam acrobat. "Who's dead?" he asked excitedly.

Vicki and I were almost as shocked by the Professor's sudden return to life as we had been by the discovery of his death. But then great waves of relief and joy washed over me, "Professor!" I exclaimed. "We thought you were dead."

Lillolman shrugged in his cute peppy way. "That's how I sleep," he said. "It scares the hell out of everybody."

He stopped and looked at me closely, as if just then

realizing that it was me he was talking to. "What are you doing here?" he asked anxiously. "I was worried about you. You're all over the headlines. The police have been here looking for you. Why did you have to kill that other doctor? Talk first. Try to settle things. Talk. Talk."

"I didn't kill anybody," I said, my voice begging him to believe me.

He scrutinized my face for a long moment, then said finally, "I knew you didn't."

Victoria broke in, "Professor, have you seen my father?"

Lillolman turned to look at her. "Father? Who are you?"

"Forgive me, Professor," I said. "This is Victoria Brisbane. Her father is Arthur Brisbane."

"Ohhhh, yes," said Lillolman, leaning over to me and whispering, "so this is the cocker's daughter."

"Professor, where's Brophy?" I asked. "It's important that we find Brophy!"

Lillolman shook his head sadly. "I'm sorry to have to say that Brophy was taken to the North Wing."

"*What?*"

"According to Montague, the poor fella suffered a terrible mental breakdown last night."

So that was why Lillolman wasn't dead. He didn't know anything.

"But Brophy's not smart enough to have a mental

breakdown," I said to him. "Don't you understand what's going on here, Professor? Montague and Diesel are keeping people here who are perfectly healthy and bleeding their families and their estates out of fortunes. They're unscrupulous, they're immoral, and they're dangerous. They've already killed three people to get what they want."

"Holy shit!" cried Lillolman. "This place is turning out to be a nut house."

Amen to that! I thought. But now we had to move fast. "The North Wing!" I shouted, hoping we'd be in time to save poor Brophy. "Come on. Let's go."

We raced down the deserted corridors and up the dimly lighted stairs to the Violent Ward. Of course, the door was locked and bolted, and of course, Nurse Diesel had the keys. I tried reaching in through the peephole to get at the inside latch, but it couldn't be done. "No good," I said. "I can't reach it. What are we going to do? How are we going to get in?"

"Wait, " said Vicki. "Maybe there's a spare key under the mat."

Lillolman and I looked at each other in disbelief. I was beginning to notice that Victoria occasionally said some very dumb things. She didn't like our reaction one bit, however, and she knelt down and reached under the mat. When her hand reappeared it was grasping a key. She stood up, brushed herself off, and with a smile of triumph handed me the prize. "Here!" she said defiantly.

If there had been time I would have kissed her.

I unlocked and unbolted the door, and the three of us walked softly down the row of cells, listening for some sign of Brophy. Near the end of the corridor I heard some muffled sounds coming from the cell on my right. I lifted off the crossbar and opened the door. There on the floor in a corner, bound and gagged, was my dear faithful sidekick.

We rushed in and got him loose. Victoria untied his legs, Lillolman his hands, and I ripped the broad band of adhesive tape off his mouth. "Where's Brisbane?" I asked breathlessly. "Where did they take him?"

"They took him to—" Brophy began to reply, but then noticed how much it hurt to have that adhesive tape ripped off. "*Yyyoooooowwww! Yyyyyiiiiiii!*" he said.

"They took him where?" I pressed him. "Where?"

Brophy gingerly patted the area around his mouth and then set himself to think. "Give me a second," he said, his brow deeply furrowed. Then his face lit up. "Norton!" he cried. "Norton's taking him up to the tower. They drugged him. They're going to throw him off and make it look like suicide."

"Oh my God!" said Victoria, and I said, "Let's go!"

We sprinted out of the Violent Ward and down the main corridor to the tower. Crashing through the door, we gaped up at the rickety old circular wooden staircase that spiralled endlessly upward toward the airy reaches of the tower's summit.

Brophy informs Victoria that her father has been taken to the tower.

"There! Look!" yelled Lillolman, and there indeed, halfway up the staircase, was the half-mustached figure of Norton dragging the semiconscious body of Vicki's father.

"Daddy! Daddy!" she screamed, and we could hear the feeble pleading response from up above us. "Victoria . . . help me. . . ."

Stouthearted and stoutheaded, Brophy leaped onto the stairs and started climbing. Lillolman was right behind him. I didn't move.

"I . . . I can't go up. . . ." I stammered. And the fact was that even looking up had almost paralyzed me.

"He's suffering from High Anxiety," Lillolman shouted down. "It strikes one out of seven."

Victoria stared at me. "High Anxiety. So that was the reason for all that commotion on the airplane."

I nodded, my eyes on the floor. "Oh God. Oh God," I moaned. "I feel like such a . . . a. . . ."

"Coward?" Vicki suggested helpfully.

The combined weight of Norton, Brisbane, Lillolman, and Brophy was greater than anything those old stairs had borne in many years, and the sound of creaking steps and straining timbers filled the air. Gasping for breath, Lillolman had to stop about halfway up. "I can't go on," he called down, clutching his chest. "I'm not a kid anymore."

Brophy, meanwhile, was gaining rapidly on Norton, whose progress was impeded by the dead weight of the semiconscious Brisbane. Not far from the top Brophy caught up with him and grabbed hold of his foot. It froze my blood to hear that all too familiar cry wafting down from above me: "I got him! I got him! I got him!"

A vicious kick in the head from Norton's other foot dislodged Brophy and sent him tumbling down the stairs. He landed in a heap near Lillolman. "I ain't got him," he announced, and then fainted.

The Professor was almost beside himself. "What are we going to do?" he wailed. "What are we going to do? He's almost at the top."

At that point everything started happening very rapidly.

Victoria said, "I've got to save him," and started up the stairs.

"No!" I said firmly. "He'll kill you. Let me."

Without thinking, I pulled her back and started to climb myself.

Almost immediately the sickness swept over me, but I kept climbing, eyes closed, body hugging the wall. Even if I got to the top, I'd be in no state to do anything by the time I arrived.

"Hurry, darling! Hurry!" Victoria called.

Each step was so much harder than the last, and each breath made me feel more dizzy. I passed Lillolman and Brophy, but I could feel the strength running out of me. This just wasn't going to work.

But it had to work! There was too much at stake for me to falter now. I kept climbing.

Thorndyke suffers an attack of High Anxiety while climbing the tower.

For two steps. The third one gave way suddenly when I put my weight on it.

I started to slide through the gap where the step had been, and only at the last instant did my hands get a clawing grip on the next step up.

And so I dangled there, fifty feet above the floor, and the red and purple spots I remembered from the phone booth reappeared before my eyes. Very shortly I would faint, and then all the pain and struggling would be over.

"Hold on! Hold on!" Lillolman yelled up to me. "Pull yourself up! You can do it!"

At the bottom of the steps Vicki was screaming, "He's going to fall! He's going to fall!"

As between "You can do it!" and "He's going to fall!" there couldn't be much doubt about which was the better bet. I could feel my fingers slipping. It would only be a few seconds now, and then peace.

"Thorndyke, listen to me!" Lillolman shouted. "I've finished my research on your case. I know what's giving you the High Anxiety. I found the answer!"

"It's too late," said one part of my brain, but another part pricked up its ears.

"Go back in your mind," said Lillolman. "Go back. You're a baby. Your mother and father are fighting. They're always fighting. They're fighting about *you!*"

My mind tumbled backward in time. Parents . . . fighting . . . parents . . . fighting . . . fighting . . . fighting . . . I was high up in the air, and my parents were fighting. I was crying in my highchair, and my parents were fighting. "I hate this kid," my father was shouting. "He's making us prisoners. We're trapped in this house. We can never go out." Then my mother was shouting back, "What do you want me to do? Get rid of him? Get rid of him? Get rid of him?" I was crying in my highchair and they were fighting and I wanted to make them stop. "Shut him up!" my father was screaming. "Shut him up! Shut him up! I can't take it!" I was crying in my highchair and I began to climb out to make them stop fighting and the highchair began to tip over. *"He's falling!"* came the sound of my mother's hysterical scream. *"HE'S FALLING!"* And I was falling—falling falling falling, until suddenly the realization hit me with a crash: I knew at last what I had always feared.

"I understand now!" I shouted as I dangled in mid-air. "I understand now! It's not heights I'm afraid of. *It's parents!"*

"Yes!" Professor Lillolman screeched. "Now climb, you son-of-a-bitch. Climb!"

Slowly, painfully, I pulled myself up onto the step I'd been hanging from. I paused there, took two deep breaths, and then began vaulting up the steps toward Norton, who, with Brisbane slung over his shoulder, was just now disappearing through the trap door onto the roof. I felt free and whole, full of courage and power, as if a great weight had been lifted off my back. I reached the trap door in less than half a minute. From above me I could hear Brisbane's tortured voice. "Whe—What—Who—Oh my God! No! No!"

I shot onto the roof. Ten yards from me, at a gap in the tower's parapet, Norton had Brisbane halfway over the edge. There was no time. A block and tackle on a long rope hung down from a hook just above me. I unhooked it and swung it hard. "Norton!" I yelled, and he turned just in time to catch it square in the face. He dropped like a stone to the floor.

Brisbane was going over, but I raced to him and pulled him back in time.

"Thank you. Thank you," he sobbed. "You saved my life."

I felt like sobbing myself. "Thank God," I said. "It's all over, Mr. Brisbane. It's all over."

But it wasn't. We heard a blood-curdling scream and turned to see Nurse Diesel flying toward us from the other side of the tower, bent on pushing us both to our doom.

Without thinking I shoved Brisbane aside and twisted out of Diesel's way. Her momentum was too great for her to stop herself. She clawed at the wall as she went through the gap, but all she could grasp was a broom that was hanging there on a nail. The small clip on the end of the broomstick held her weight for half a second, but then it snapped off. She plummeted down toward the rocky surf far below us, straddling the broomstick and screaming like the wicked witch from Snow White.

Norton (Lee Delano) just about to get rid of Arthur Brisbane (Albert Whitlock).

Now it was really over. Montague emerged from the shadows with his hands up in the air and his fingers crossed. *"Fins!"* he snivelled. *"Fins.* I give up. I give up. I never liked her. I never *really* liked her."

Vicki, Brophy, and Lillolman burst through the trap door and looked wildly around. Then Vicki saw her father and ran to his side.

"My baby, oh, my baby," Brisbane cried as he hugged her close.

"Daddy. Daddy. I love you," Victoria said.

A bit over-stimulated by all this, Brophy leaped up and threw his arms around. "My boss. My boss," he gurgled.

"Take it easy, fella," I said.

I turned to Professor Lillolman and vigorously shook his hand. "Thank you, Professor. You did it. You saved my life."

"Hah!" Lillolman barked. "And they say we charge too much."

Vicki's father came over to me. "You saved my life," he said. "Who are you?"

But it was Vicki who answered. "That's the fella I'm going to marry."

And that was the fella she did marry. We've been blissfully happy ever since.

Norton and Montague were both sentenced to long terms in prison, where they are now both safely locked up.

Diesel attempts to kill Thorndyke and Arthur Brisbane.

Victoria announces her marital intentions to Thorndyke.

Victoria and Thorndyke on a "surprise" honeymoon.

Lillolman, at my urging, agreed to accept the job of Associate Director of the P-NIV,VN, and as I write this he is in his office across the hall treating one of our patients.

Brophy is still the Institute's driver, but thanks to his famous front-page picture of "me," he now also has a part-time job as an apprentice photographer with a large metropolitan newspaper.

Nurse Diesel is dead.

Almost certainly.